THOUGHT
&
OTHER ABSURDITIES

VOLUME 2

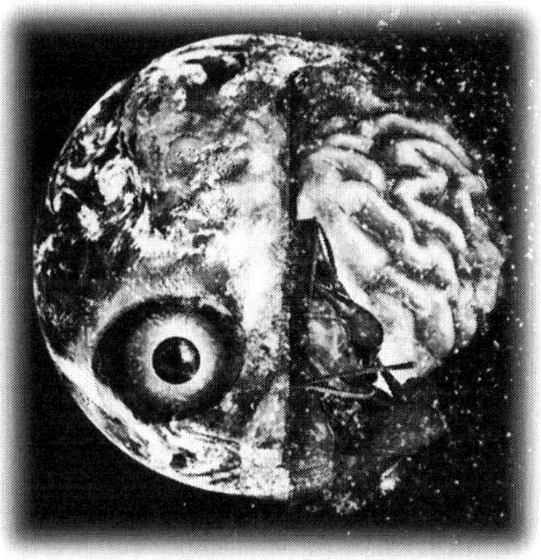

JOSEPH D. NEWCOMER

DEAD
STAR
PRESS

ISBN: 978-1-955623-09-4

ACKNOWLEDGMENTS

&

DEDICATIONS

For those of you who find solace in the knowledge that some of us acknowledge the same disastrous and seemingly endless satire of horrors that is life. May you enjoy its greatest trivialities despite playing your role in continuing the infinitely disturbing and, at times, beautifully comedic tragedy of it all.

&

My Family

Andrea Greenwald & Ariella Nova Newcomer

Thank you for your support.

William and Stacey Hetrick, Forrest Shaw, Shaf, Lee Edmondson, David Johnson, DAJO, TJ, The Ottenas, Trevor Huster, Jared White, Zachary Short, Sperry Hutchinson, Sebastien Reyes, Stuart Shoen, Katie Turk, Nikki Behr, The Greenwalds, Turkos, McCalls, Ciminos, Colemans, Wokutches, Sousaes, Bruinsmas, Kuligowskis, Trohoskes, Reists, Wertheims, Whitleys, Corban Ford, Adonnis Blake, Andrew Dady, Jason Bean, Chris Donley, Dan Scamell, Brett Thomas, J. Edward Young, Cyril Serenissima, Charles Passman, Michael Mayes, Chelsea Harrington, Howard Gershkowitz, Edwin Canfield, Beau Montana, Ken Brown & Drawn to Comics, Werner Books, Phoenix Magazine, Sylvia and David Newcomer,

& Fucking…Me.

1. The Inner Voice of Treason

1.25.21

Hey guys, go ahead and hang the toilet paper any way you want, buy it all up, order a steak well done and put ketchup on it, double-dip your chips, use than and then like they are interchangeable—your and you're and there, their, and they're, too or to, if you prefer, and leave your grocery cart anywhere you like. Nothing matters anymore. Nothing is simply understood. Everything is debatable. Everything is a conspiracy. Only you are right. Only what matters to you is important. You do you. Live your life with reckless abandon. Only hear what you want to hear. Only see what you want to see. You might not be in good company, but you'll certainly be in ample company.

A few idiots who believe they have the power to speak for everyone have spoken.

deflection. What I honestly feel is an addition to my compounding loss. I will miss my friend. I will always wonder who the dead girl was before she pulled the trigger. These are my burdens, not theirs. These selfish notions are not useful thoughts by which to base their character. You can't decide how other people should feel and then be disappointed in them for not feeling the way you decided they should, but we all do it. Other people are not you, you shouldn't want them to be, it's not possible, and you wouldn't like them if they were.

While it would be easy to write them off for their choices simply because I disagree with them, the harder thing to do is to understand, to allow myself

2. Ether of Us

4.8.21

One of the most naturally decent parts of our nature happens when we experience something so wonderfully intoxicating to our existence that we are immediately compelled to share it with others. This is how we connect in the ether when it seems increasingly impossible that we should be able to do so.

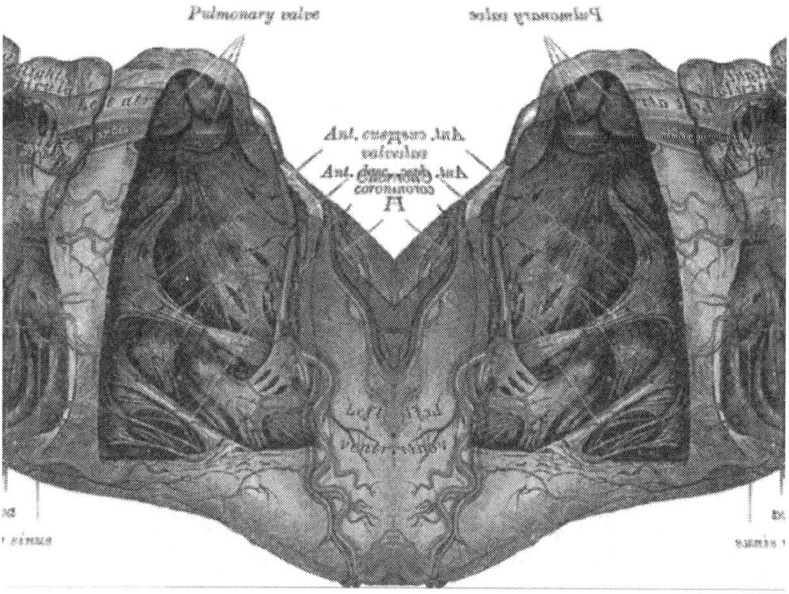
Pulmonary valve

3. The Nude Colossus

4.23.21

The sentiments of old poems on old statues have been abandoned. Once, they filled patriots with rightful pride, but that pride is now only ego, and the meaning of the symbol is lost on nationalists who ignorantly boast of their allegiance to an idol they are unable to understand. The plain language, as esoteric as a child's textbook, could only ever be misinterpreted by a mind intent on twisting—by a mind intent on excusing itself of all wrong—by the graceless mind of cowardice.

Be decent and compassionate and empathetic, beyond semantics, beyond policy, beyond law, beyond your self-serving, bullshit agenda.

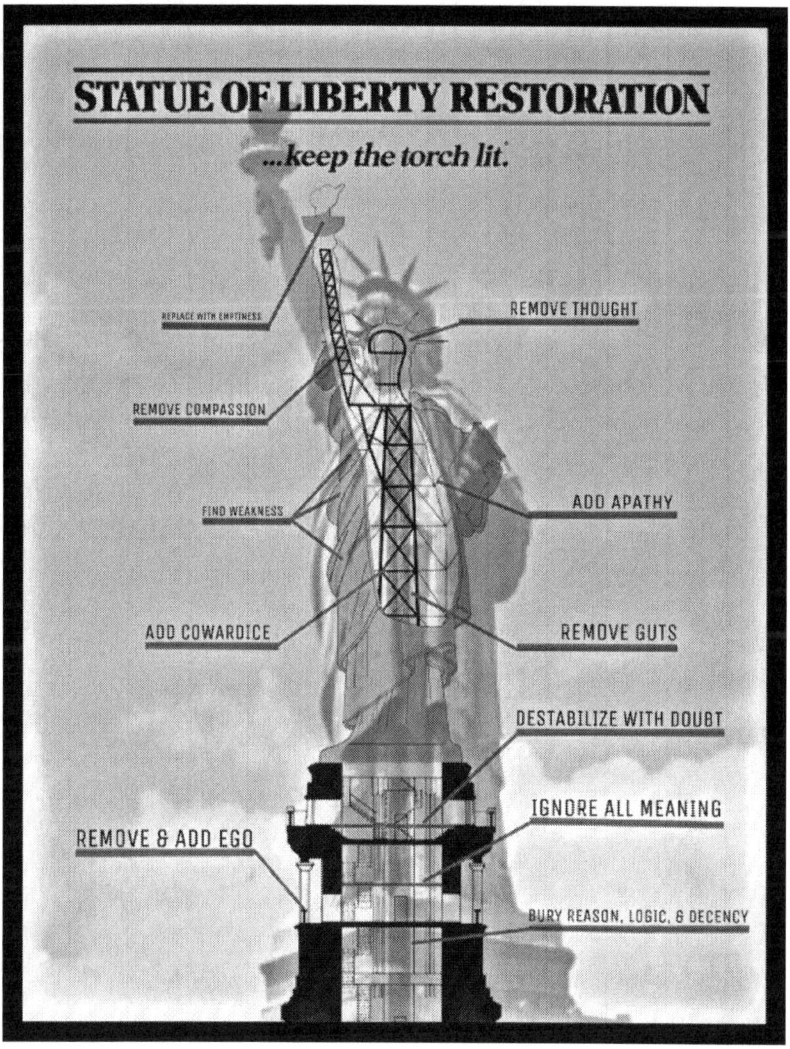
STATUE OF LIBERTY RESTORATION
...keep the torch lit.
REPLACE WITH EMPTINESS
REMOVE THOUGHT
REMOVE COMPASSION
FIND WEAKNESS
ADD APATHY
ADD COWARDICE
REMOVE GUTS
DESTABILIZE WITH DOUBT
IGNORE ALL MEANING
REMOVE & ADD EGO
BURY REASON, LOGIC, & DECENCY

4. Idol Man is the Devil Aground

4.30.21

We have no needs, no real drive, and we can't be bothered to understand this passion in others. We are full bellies in a grocery store, unaffected by desire. And so, we stagnate in boredom and ennui, hoping to find the intangible thing that we feel we're missing, which is our want for a need, for a purpose. We tire of having the world at our fingertips without a meaningful reason to fight for anything. Weakened with privilege, we trouble ourselves with finding other reasons while progress stalls in wasted abundance.

5. One Man's Trash is Another Man's Terminus (A Litter Nation)

5.7.21

The year is 2022, and humanity is nearly snuffed out by the mountainous blankets of irresponsibly discarded, infectious disease prevention masks. In the narrow pathways between towering mask mounds, the few children still in existence play a darkly amended version of Rock, Paper, Scissors called Covid, Climate Change, Crushed by Maskalanche. The viral epidemic was just the beginning. It was exponentially worsened by humanity's lack of concern for the environment.

Once the great scare hit, it was already too late. After the first few rounds of panic buying, the grocery stores were forced to turn people away in droves. There were still food goods and other necessities inside, but there was just no parking because the apathetic littering didn't stop at masks. Every parking space was filled with mid-lot-abandoned shopping carts. The cart returners just couldn't keep up, and decent humans, Good Samaritans with brain-enough to return the carts to the proper areas, mere feet away, were few and entirely outnumbered, not that it would have helped. There were just so many masks. There was no escaping them, nowhere to go, nowhere to sleep, nowhere to eat, and it probably wasn't even a good idea to breathe.

(Please, wear your masks when it is appropriate, or don't, no one is going to change anyone's mind about that, but for the love of the Robot Overlords, don't throw them on the fucking ground.)

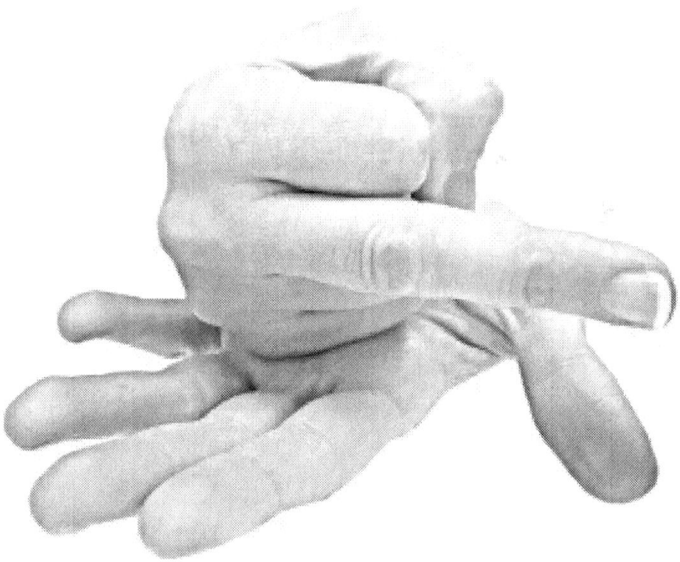

6. Subjugation Ruling the Nation

5.11.21

I wonder about the type of person or entity that would be interested in grand declarations of faith, love, and loyalty. I wonder, and I imagine that a human, creature, or deity requiring such displays would be undeserving of them for the same reasons they require them. We are not the things that are demanded of us, not the people we feel we are demanded to be by anyone or any thing. In fact, we are most the thing that we would be had nothing been asked of us, expected of us, or demanded of us in the first place.

NO
KNEELING
GROVELING
ALLEGIANCE
NO SERVICE

7. Know Fear

5.18.21

It may seem impressive and brave when someone claims not to be afraid of anything, but it is more likely that they've suffered severe brain damage to one or both of their amygdalae. If you find yourself lacking the natural human emotion meant to ensure that you take the proper steps to preserve your life in dangerous scenarios, instead of bragging about it on social media, you should probably see a neurologist. A certain amount of fear is necessary, healthy, and normal.

Be afraid. Be a very reasonable amount of afraid.

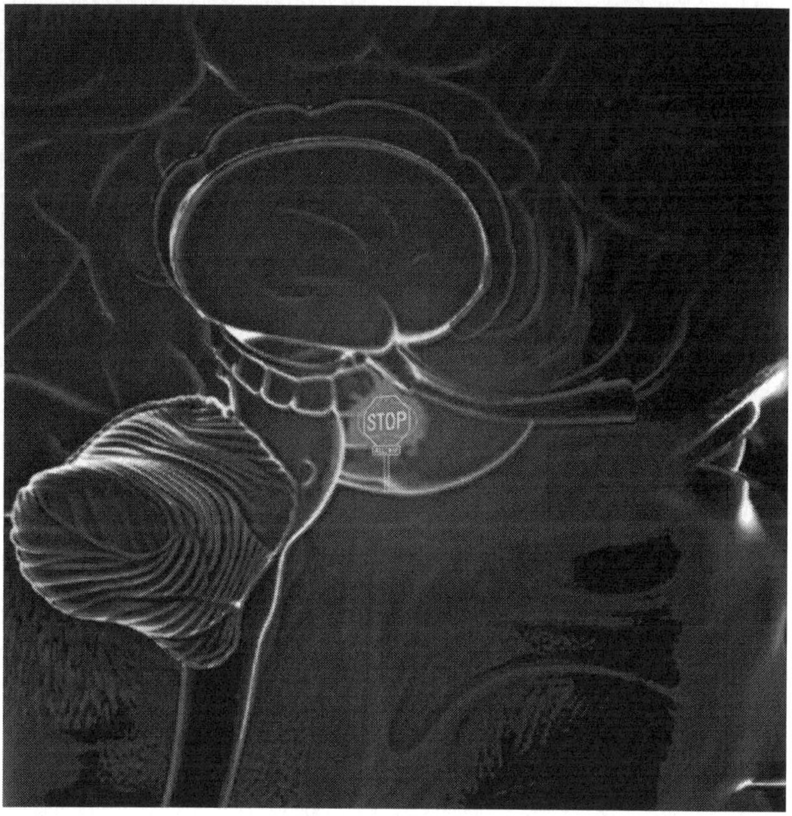
STOP

8. Dog God (Jesus on Paper Part II)

5.26.21

Presently, the value of any type of currency is based on faith—no one less arbitrary than another. "This is money, this is what has value, and this is how it works. Other things can't be this." That is the lesson we are taught. It has no merit, but we see it in practice, and we believe in it without question. It fails when we stop believing because that is the only thing that made it true.

9. Haute Box

6.8.21

Many social groups are just as pretentious as those that boldly claim to be. Sometimes, those who seem as though they should be the most open-minded are the same amount of pseudo-pretentious. It's mostly because people are insecure, and we struggle with our need to belong. Once we feel we belong, we need to reinforce our desire to be seen as important/accepted, which, again, all stems from a lack of self-importance and the overwhelming desire to feel validated. The power to exclude others makes us feel that importance. It elevates us in our own imaginary position of social status. It's sad and pathetic and all very human. This is not to say that these groups have no value; the gathering of like-minded individuals to benefit a cause or purpose can certainly be effective and beneficial for all of its members, it's just that the lesser parts of our nature often overshadow any value.

If you are part of one of these groups, it may be beneficial to reevaluate the true nature of why you are and how it has affected your treatment of outsiders. Just because this is a very understandable and natural way to behave, it's still not a particularly great justification for doing so.

If you've been excluded, consider yourself lucky not to be wanted by groups or individuals who are these types of things.

Being excluded from a social group can be a higher honor than being accepted.

The best part of being a shape that doesn't fit in the box is not getting put in a box.

10. The Ire in Irony

6.15.21

Someone posts a video of themselves doing something stupid, entitled, wasteful, and repulsive enough to be embarrassing for all humankind. We share it to tell people just how disgusted we are by it, and we laugh the laughs of subconscious desperation. The person who posted it gets a million more views because of our shares, and they are paid for those views by advertisers and social media channels.

We have just participated in furthering the stupidity of our culture. We need to stop sharing, reacting, and commenting on things we hate, no matter how much our blood boils. It's up to us to stop perpetuating this trash, to not give these idiots a voice or a platform or more of the new, most powerful monetary unit—views. We need to remove ourselves from this equation, from being part of the problem. If everyone did it for six months, these horrible videos would no longer be profitable, and they would stop.

"And America wonders why people hate us. These assholes just wasted sixty dollars on candy and soda or spaghetti and meatballs so they could get a few views on

YouTube. We really need to stop sharing stuff like this and start thinking about how sick these people really are and how much we are enabling them by sharing it."

-Me ranting like a stubborn old man yelling at children on his lawn to my poor significant other.

11. HGTV Barbie

6.22.21

In my opinion, the Barbie Dreamhouse bathroom is a huge waste of square footage. I mean, not a single one of the dolls has a butthole. And while we're at it, get rid of the kitchen. These people can't eat. Their mouths don't even open. Christ, use all of that extra space to make the tiny ass pool bigger. Barbie barely fits in the pool by herself. How in the hell are Skipper and Chelsea supposed to get into it, too? Honestly, though, I guess they don't really even need a house at all.

-Thoughts you have when you start losing imagination to age, and you write social commentary, but you also have a four-year-old, and you're a new homeowner.

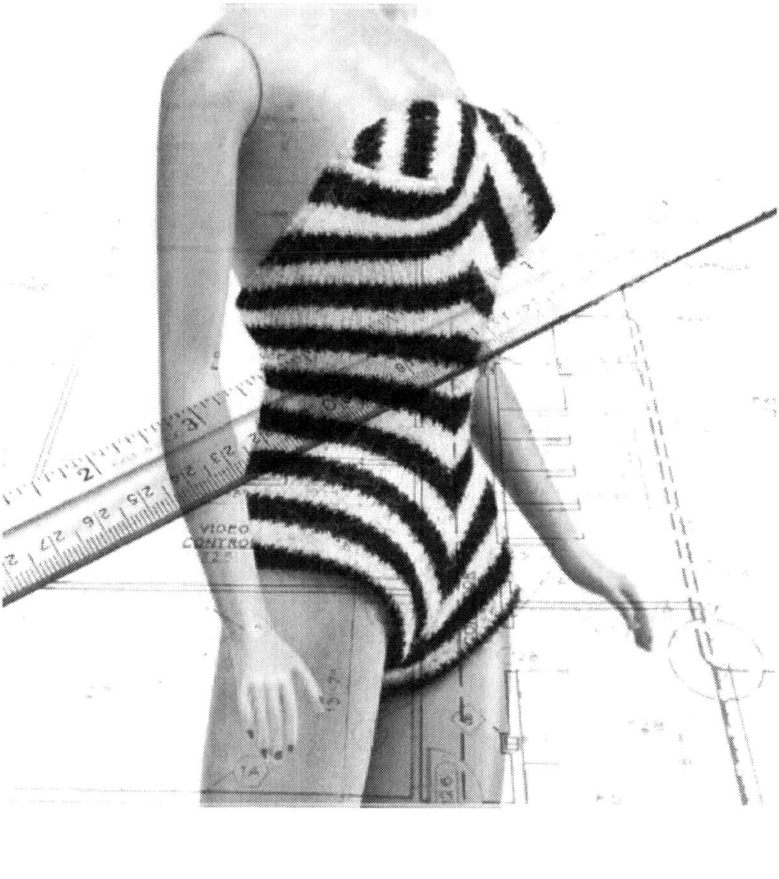

12. Thoughts From Inside a Crumbling Society: Volume III

7.2.21

I'll have the literacy with extra cheese and pepperoni.

If they made retro Pizza Huts with red cups, jukeboxes, a couple of video games, and a pizza buffet, and ran BOOK IT! promotions for adults, it would change the world.

Back then, the red cup was still only half-full, but there were refills in the pitchers.

. . .

I think we are developed enough as a country, nay as a species, to ban the manufacturing of single-ply, printer-paper-hard toilet paper. It's time.

. . .

Thinking about how much different The Beatles' song, A Day in the Life, would be if it were written today.

"I read the news today. Oh, fuck!"

. . .

When I run out of ridiculous shit to write about, I just

read the news.

. . .

PSA: There's a video of Cardi B explaining how to clean your butt. I'm not suggesting you watch it or do what she says because I'm a believer in "For external use only" warnings, but I think it's vital to know it's out there. Teach your kids how to clean their butts, or Cardi B will.

. . .

Some days, I think, when am I going to stop screwing around with all of these other foods and just eat garlic bread exclusively? I'm tired of living this lie.

. . .

Sunday could be the best day of the week if we were better at compartmentalizing.

. . .

It's all fun and games until reality gets broken.

. . .

I'm always impressed by how easy it is for really stupid people to quickly break down and simplify a complex issue that they couldn't possibly understand. It's like they don't even have to think about it at all.

Simple people think everything is simple.

Thanks for making it make sense for the rest of us average individuals by throwing out absurdly cliché sayings. I guess it really is what it is. Thank you, genius.

. . .

With each new day comes a new opportunity to lie to yourself about how much better it will be.

-Unmotivational Life Coach Quote of the Day

. . .

After spending a little time on the internet, you start to notice how gross it is when people act happy and pretend that they like each other.

. . .

Stupid environment, always making it difficult to be irresponsible. Who needs it?

. . .

The best way to get people behind a horrible idea is to convince them that it's the only option.

-American politics

. . .

Fun Fact:

Human pupils are really just black holes that are slowly sucking all of the light out of the universe.

. . .

Some people use public restroom toilet seat covers to protect themselves. Some should clearly be using them to protect the toilet.

. . .

Not being able to go into a Blockbuster Video on a Friday night still doesn't sit well with me.

. . .

This is America! *Everyone is innocent until proven guilty.

*Excludes people with opposing political, societal, & religious views

. . .

Look, I don't care if people are ignorant pieces of shit in the privacy of their own home, but I don't need it thrown in my face constantly on TV & Facebook. I mean, what am I supposed to say to my kid when she sees you being a stupid bigot?

. . .

Just saw a post where a person got shit on for openly engaging in conversations & listening to all sides of issues without condemning any of them so that people could hear all of the info & form their own opinions. It was the Internetiest.

. . .

It's very confusing that people are willing to give certain people whom they do not know the benefit of the doubt over people they know well.

. . .

I love when we try to discredit something, and we start with, "I just don't understand..." As if our inability to comprehend it makes it impossible. Maybe we're just dumb.

. . .

I follow the strict ideology of a particular political party, so I really don't have to think or be rational. I just consult the manual with the rest of the mob.

. . .

Had you read more Sci-Fi, you would know how predictably people are behaving.

. . .

The most encouraging part of all the horrific news I've read today is that we must be getting closer to the end.

-The power of positivity.

. . .

The best part of being wrong is finding all of the people online who agree with you.

. . .

Ugh! Really? People actually still believe in stuff? How exhausting! I mean, why?

. . .

Ugh! People are still saying things to other people? I thought we made the Internet so we didn't have to do that anymore.

. . .

The easiest way to figure out if someone is an asshole

is to hold a mirror up to their face. If the mirror steams up, they're an asshole.

. . .

People are calling bullets "freedom seeds."

How are we not extinct?

. . .

More often than not, when a person tries to convince you how simple and clear-cut a truly complex problem really is, they are trying to sell you something.

. . .

Looking into this "Freedom" stuff, and there's a hell of a lot of paperwork and fine print.

. . .

One of my favorite things about social media is that while we have as much time as we'd like to think and form a response, most of us still just type the first dumb thing that comes to our minds.

. . .

The weirdest thing you could ever wish to be is "normal."

. . .

I'm not sighing. You're sighing.

. . .

If our faces were honest, we'd all have RBF.

. . .

If you're not in a good mood today, it may be due to the fact that children's movies gave all of us very unrealistic expectations of the exciting and fun relationships people have with their pets.

. . .

In your youth, you often think about how unfair life is. As an adult, you realize just how right you were. Then you get a pimple inside your nose.

. . .

Sometimes it's nice to wake up an hour before your alarm clock goes off, so you can just lie there and think about stuff.

-No One Ever

. . .

So many arguments really come down to one or more people choosing to exercise their right to be complete fucking assholes.

. . .

Me: (shakes phone) OK, Facebook, are we living in fear today, or are we not letting fear control us?

Facebook: Reply hazy. Try again.

. . .

Humanity could be such a beautiful thing if it weren't for all the humans.

. . .

I find it fascinating that people feel the need to specify it as "doom scrolling, " as if there's any other kind of scrolling.

. . .

Hell is trying to be happy.

. . .

Ever mention how people are so stupid, and someone else chimes in, "OMFG, YES!" and then they rattle off a list of things stupid people do, and you do every one of them, and think, *"This person is so stupid"*?

. . .

America would benefit from a more rewards-based system. Like, "Wow! You didn't kill anyone today. Here's some pie. Don't forget, if you can make it the whole year, you get an extra week of vacation!"

. . .

Reading actual literature is the vaccine for our societal ills. Unfortunately, some of those who need it most refuse to get it.

. . .

Do you ever think about how much simpler life would be if you could make other people's heads explode with your mind?

. . .

The answer to either/or can, and sometimes should, be neither/nor.

. . .

If you're in a good mood in the morning, you should know that I assume that either you're a sociopath or you've just eaten bacon.

. . .

Don't waste your time or energy being disappointed in yourself for not succeeding with your creativity. You're going to need those things for being disappointed in the world for not getting it, while you keep being creative.

. . .

If you're getting defensive for your political party when someone says (non-politically) that we should all try to stop being bigoted assholes, maybe you should find a new political party.

. . .

We're probably all just being punished for picking our noses in the shower.

. . .

I read that in order to be successful, you sometimes just need to redefine success.

Binge-watching Sci-Fi shows, eating snacks, and napping is now success. You're welcome.

. . .

No matter how shitty things are going for you, never forget to take a few moments out of your crappy life to criticize others for trying to do something with theirs.

. . .

Familiarity breeds contempt. We should all try not speaking to each other.

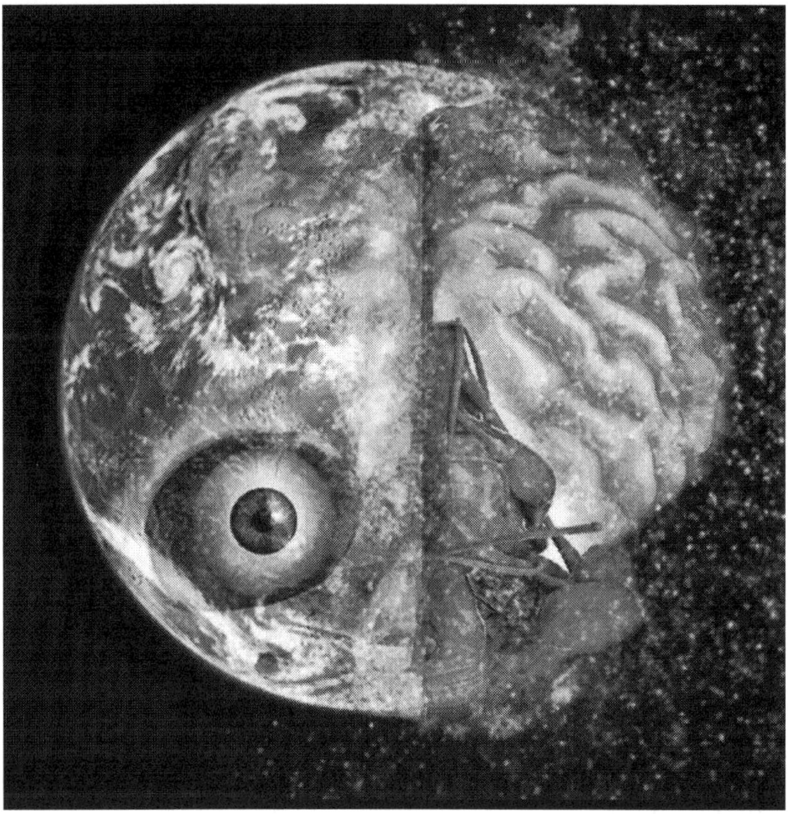

13. For Love of the Shame

7.15.21

Living is a terribly humiliating proposition. If you make it through a single day without embarrassing yourself or feeling mortified for someone else, you've absolutely beaten the odds. It's all a very telling sign that so few of us are able to do the things we feel we are meant to do, and instead, we only get to do what we are forced by our needs to do—things that feel unnatural to us so that we are able sustain a life in this humiliating world we've constructed.

Consider the weary traveler. They have a lot on their mind, trying to get to the airport through traffic, thinking and hoping they haven't forgotten something at their house or in the hotel, wondering if they'll be able to get to their gate in time because their kid was screaming all morning and wouldn't brush their teeth, so now they're running late, just praying that the bag of drugs doesn't break open in their colon.

Now, they're at security, and they have to suffer the indignity of flubbing up a simple pleasantry because the TSA agent is going to say, "Have a nice flight," and our distracted, broken, human traveler is, without a doubt, going to say, "You too," and feel like a complete ass for at least the next thirty minutes, possibly, the rest of their day, probably, for the rest of their life.

This is how we are humbled, by tiny fractures in our egos. This is what frames the self-confidence of even the most eloquent and confident of our kind. We all say and do stupid shit. If we all could allow ourselves to acknowledge it, this fact should moderate our most arrogant and reassure the meekest.

14. Fame Fatale

7.22.21

One of the difficulties of life in the present is that everyone knows that they're really only one viral video away from fame, riches, and stardom. Generations before us saw those things as pipe dreams that only the most resilient could even begin to think of as achievable, so settling for something believed to be lesser wasn't the worst fate imaginable. Now, with the perceived ease of wild, undeserved success staring us all in the back of our phones, when we aren't able to achieve what seems so reasonably attainable, life seems even more cruel and unusual. Perhaps this is part of the reason so very many of us feel dissatisfied.

15. Rhetoric Necrotic

7.27.21

We are tirelessly consumed by our opinions and how we must prove them to be right until all else is lost. In the end, we are only left tired and angry for never having proved them to be right.

Agreeing to disagree is just agreeing with yourself that you disagree with the other person because they are obviously wrong.

-Internet Arguing 101

3
3
ETHOS
PATHOS
LOGOS

16. Pavlov's Sisyphus

8.5.21

Remember that year when most of us had to spend as much time at home as we normally spend at work, and most of us were all so brainwashed into thinking that all of our worth was based on work, and that our passions could only be hobbies, and that this new dynamic was just impossibly uncomfortable and wrong, that we went crazy and were super angry instead of realizing that life actually should be like that all of the time?

-Questions for the not-distant-enough future.

17. Cart Wheel in the Produce Section

8.11.21

Paraphrasing real life:

Cashier: "Would you like to join our preferred customer shopping club?"

Me: "Sure, maybe. What's that do for me?"

Cashier: "Well, you would get exclusive promotional savings and discounts."

Me: "So I just use this card, and I get money off my groceries."

Cashier: "Exactly!"

Me: "Great! Sign me up."

(Gives the cashier personal information, then waits for him to scan the groceries and the new Preferred Shopper's Club Card.)

Me: "Wait. Why didn't I get any discounts?"

Cashier: "Oh, well, you have to download our app and scroll through and select which discounts you'd like to have applied to your card."

Me: "All of them, I'd like all of the discounts. Can I just do that?"

Cashier: "Unfortunately, that's not how it works."

Me: "But aren't I a preferred customer?"

Cashier: "Yes, and we prefer our customers to download our app and spend hours looking through hundreds of possible discounts and advertising rather than doing any of the billion things they'd prefer to be doing."

Me: "What do I get if I don't do that?"

Cashier: "Sir, I already gave you the card."

Every week, for at least an hour, we get to make a thousand stressful, panic-inspiring decisions. We make split-second, risk-reward analyses that force us to weigh our finances against the health, safety, and future of our families, trying to predict if we're even going to have enough energy to cook what we're buying, knowing the whole time that all of the Produce may as well go directly into the trash, and all while fighting a rogue wheel of death on the front of our carts that's trying desperately to slam us into the coolers, other shopper's carts, and small, passing children. At the end of the hour, there is a brief moment when we look at our carts and think to ourselves, "I really think I nailed it this week. There's no way this can be over a hundred dollars." Then they ring us up, and it's two hundred sixty. We reluctantly pay. Then we wrestle with the cart like we're steering a ten-speed through a gravel quarry for the mile to the car, even though all three hundred spots right outside the doors are empty because they're reserved for people who are wise enough to do online orders for pick-up.

My favorite Comedian, Forrest Shaw, said it best.

"They're still making you make decisions on your health, based on money. We shouldn't have to do that, but we're in the store, and we're like, OK, I can get the organic grapes for twenty dollars, or I can get the grapes for a dollar, ninety-nine sprayed with poison. I'm going with the poison grapes. I've got to pay rent. Bag 'em up!"

18. As Seen In Dreams

8.20.21

We have an expanding working knowledge of how to modify the contents of our dreams. Soon, our subconscious will be commodified. The blank space of our sleep, the billboards of the future, we are the opportunity-product to be bought and sold, to be vied for in a race for financial superiority. We will rest, but only physically. Our consumer brains will continue on, traversing the nightmarish landscapes of perpetual marketing, and when we wake, we will buy, baby! Buy, buy, buy.

It is already our reality—faceless, profiting intermediaries selling time slots of our lives, bits of our existence (something that's simply not theirs to sell) as impression-potential to the highest bidder, and for that which we should be generously compensated, we only happily beg to pay more for our victimization.

As we've grown so accustomed to saying, take my money.

AS SEEN IN DREAMS

19. Passé the Time

9.7.21

A broken clock is right twice a day. A clock that works but is set to the wrong time may never be correct.

Everything we've created in this world is a distraction from the pain of wanting to know things we simply cannot know. Now, distractions are all we have, so enjoy them. Choose those that fulfill you over those that only offer grief and aggravation.

We mostly judge each other on how we choose to waste/spend our time. I write speculative science fiction with social commentary because there are so many things in life that I wish weren't real–the things we see every day but for which we can't find logical explanations. I try to give them reasons–closure. It's not unlike how I imagine the gods were invented.

20. Miring in Admiration

9.14.21

The pain of admiration, awareness, appreciation, and knowledge is understanding the beauty of something someone created and realizing that you may never enjoy something of your own as much.

This is what I think when I read Kurt Vonnegut, or Philip K. Dick, or listen to the lyrics of Sean Nelson of Harvey Danger.

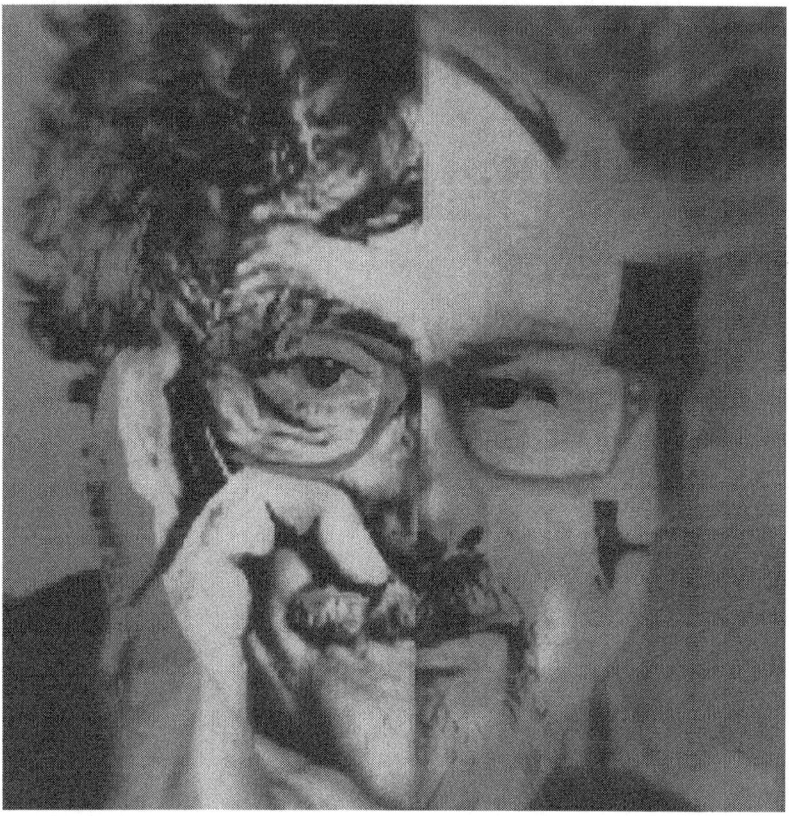

21. Self on the Shelf

9.21.21

As the world is seemingly sucked into the black-hole-vacuum of despair around us, we are faced with a new self-punishment. It is guilt above all, in glorious, Old Testament abundance, when we consider our own suffering. We've added a personal, internal attack for our sadness when it is directed inward. It's as if we've disallowed any sympathetic emotion unless it is being extended to others. No matter the circumstances of our failures, regardless of how we relentlessly worked toward our goals, despite how justified we are for feeling the slightest pity for our own existence, we convince ourselves that these thoughts—this compassion for ourselves is categorically wrong because there is such great suffering outside of us—that there are far greater travesties and tragedies to be prioritized. While all of these significant targets for our empathy may be more deserving, the importance of our need for internal sympathy cannot be diminished or overstated. I truly believe that without it, we take the final step in the dissolution of our universally deteriorating mental health. It's okay to feel bad for yourself. It makes you no less aware of or affected by the suffocating swell of justified depression of those who surround you. There are no limits to our mercy in either direction.

22. Freudian Slap

9.28.21

If America had a therapist, they would probably tell it to try not to make any more major life decisions until it's feeling less emotional. Maybe try some meditation, or yoga, a healthier diet, and maybe some exercise. They might say it wouldn't be a bad idea to start each day with about twenty-four hours of quiet self-reflection.

23. Kenny Rogers Roasted

10.5.21

For this all to work as designed, it must operate like a casino. It's predicated on the fact that most of us will lose and just keep putting more into the machine. The machine empties into one pocket. Money and happiness flow upward, and work and misery flow down.

Kenny Rogers was mistaken. You never had a choice in the first place. There is no holding or folding, and you can't walk away, let alone run. You are, however, on a train bound for nowhere, but you're in the engine car with everyone else, shoveling your soot-black soul into the furnace to keep the machine moving toward its nowhere destination.

JOKER
JOKER

24. The Jawbone of an Asshole

10.12.21

If you are confused and unsure who to trust, I hope this will be helpful. The easy answer is no one. And that may be entirely true, but you still have to make decisions based on the available information. In politics, as is in the rest of life, you can only really trust a person of reasonably sound mind to do the thing that they feel is going to save their own ass or to allow them to be successful in whatever it is that they do.

Imagine a car salesman who works at an economy brand and price dealership. Imagine he tells you about how the economy brand car he is trying to sell you is the best make and model on the road. So, you buy the car. The next day, you pull up next to him at a red light. He's driving a car that is not the make and model you purchased. He's actually driving a much more expensive foreign model—one he told you was a waste of your money and that your car was a much better vehicle than. His true opinion is that the car he purchased is better, but he doesn't benefit from telling you the truth.

On the other hand, let's say he does work at the

dealership that actually sells the best possible quality make and model of car, and he tells you this, and it's the truth. So, you purchase that car. You bought the best car, yes, but he only told you the truth out of convenience because it's what benefits him most. This is the same across the board in most scenarios. It's a cliché for a reason. Pay attention to what people do, give much less regard to what they say to you.

25. Introverted Inverted

10.19.21

If you are an introvert or have social anxiety issues in actual life, but you are able to talk about it on social media, where millions of people can see your thoughts, you should know that's a pretty big step for you. And here's the clincher—people aren't a quarter as judgmental in real life as they are online. Way fewer people are going to be as harsh about your thoughts to your face than they will be in the comments. When someone can see your face, the innate empathy that goes along with being a human in a human interaction takes over, and perhaps that's why people can be so callous online. So, if you can do it online, you're braver than you would be to do it in real life.

PS, I think you're also doing a huge service to other people with similar feelings. It's not just misery that loves company. Even if you prefer to be alone, I would imagine that it's nice to know you're not alone in that preference.

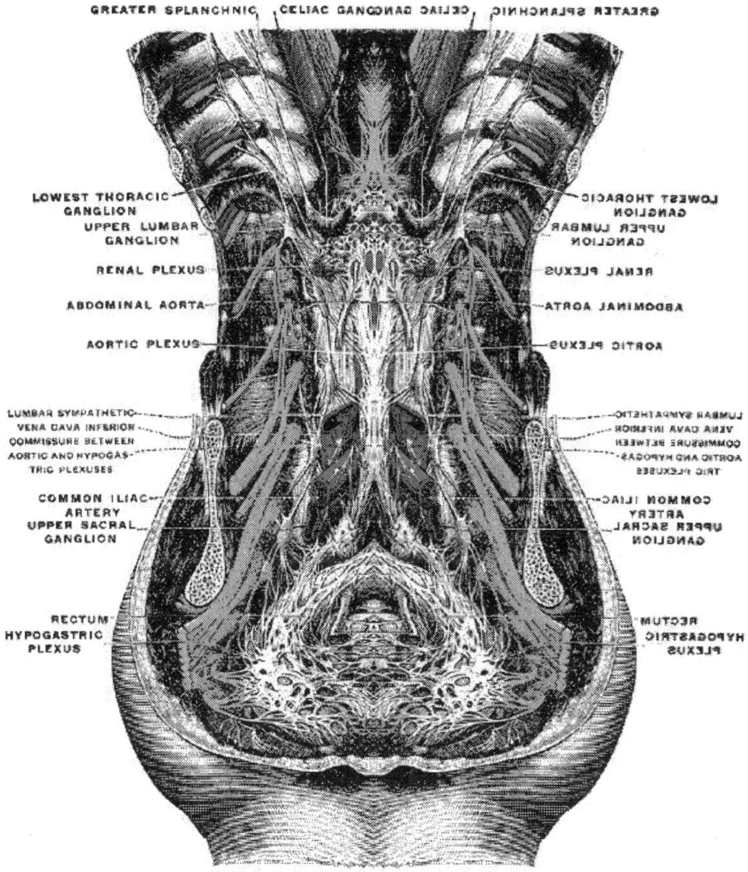
GREATER SPLANCHNIC
CELIAC GANG
LOWEST THORACIC GANGLION
UPPER LUMBAR GANGLION
RENAL PLEXUS
ABDOMINAL AORTA
AORTIC PLEXUS
LUMBAR SYMPATHETIC
VENA CAVA INFERIOR
COMMISSURE BETWEEN AORTIC AND HYPOGASTRIC PLEXUSES
COMMON ILIAC ARTERY
UPPER SACRAL GANGLION
RECTUM
HYPOGASTRIC PLEXUS

26. Unfathomable Versions: Version 2

10.26.21

I recently thought about an earlier post, entitled "Unfathomable Versions," because I encountered a situation that was very much the same as what inspired that post. I had an online discussion with someone whom I know is reasonably well educated and intellectual. His ideas and points are rooted in rationality, but his compassionless and demeaning approach toward people who disagree with him on a variety of subjects is impossible to avoid.

Unfortunately, the more patient you try to be with these personalities, the more opportunities you give them to do exactly what it is that they do. For those who choose, or perhaps are simply doomed to be this way, the discussion will more often than not turn into two arguments. The first is the argument they are having with you to get you to agree with them across the board. They insist on nothing but absolute forfeiture of any deviation from the way they feel or think. The other argument is the one in which you are pushing for them to be respectful and decent to people who disagree with them.

Should you push back with the type of aggression they brought to the conversation from the start (most likely in a passive-aggressive manner to goad you into this banal battle because they so desperately need interaction, and this is the only way they have left to get someone to have a conversation with them) the aggressive nature of the conversation will now be pinned on you. Gaslighting is the popular terminology.

When dealing with individuals who are stuck in this loop, people who know no other way of interacting, the battle becomes one of you attempting to retain any shred of respect for them. Unfortunately, for both people, it's highly unlikely. Eventually, and perhaps after a great deal of torture for the strongest-willed and most caring, you will tire of your efforts and cut these people out of your life. I've paid attention when these situations have happened. It seems that these tendencies are rarely isolated. If you examine these unfortunate souls, you will often find a pattern. They drive even the most patient of individuals out of their lives, including those who very much agree with their ideas and opinions.

You see, being right makes you no less of an asshole. It doesn't matter how intelligent or well-read or how easily you figure things out, or how revered you are for your intellect, if you haven't learned that it's more important to be kind. Until you do, you are simply dumb and emotionally inept. And you will be alone, and you will be as right as anyone who has no one to disagree with them.

I recall writing the original piece because of a previous conversation I had that was similar to this sad situation. It's much shorter than the explanation I've just given you. It's possibly a bit redundant at this point, and this whole thing could probably be easily summed up by saying, "Just don't be an asshole," but here is the original post, Unfathomable Versions.

How much you know or learn is not a measure of your depth.

Depth resides in remembering and empathizing with who and how you were before you knew what you now know—before you learned how valid or invalid what you believed is. And doing so while giving the same respect to the limitless versions of what you could have been or could never be. What you know is simply not as important as your willingness to understand the things that you do not.

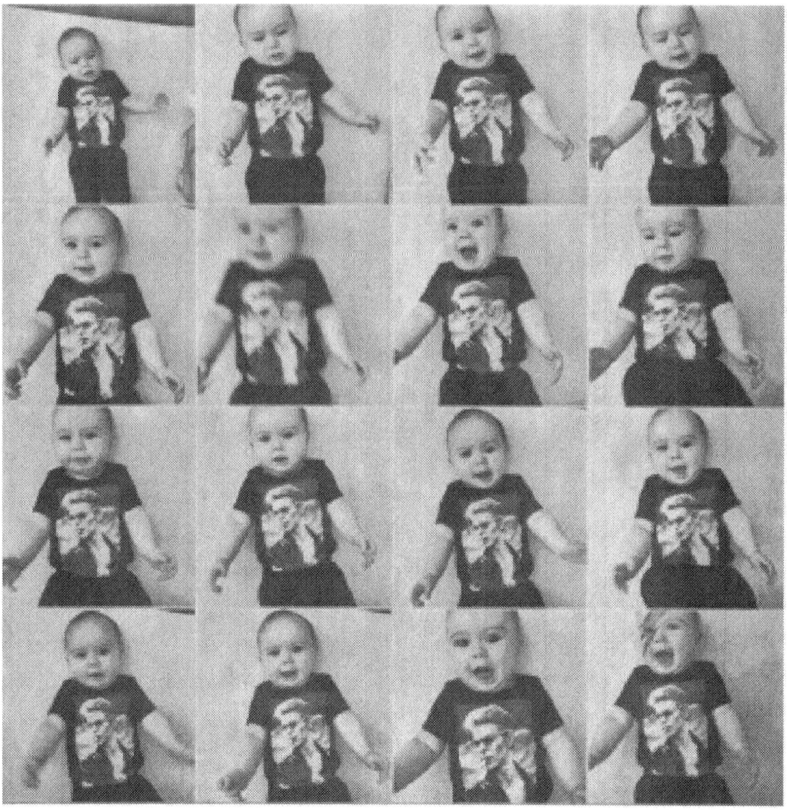

27. That Good Shit

11.2.21

We are inescapably drawn to oversimplifying ourselves and others, even though we know how incredibly complex who and what we are truly is. It's easier for us to put things into two groups, so we can make decisive choices to define ourselves. It's rarely, if ever, accurate or useful.

I try not to subscribe to either/ors. When at all possible, I also enjoy making these choices absurd or impossible to feel good about having to choose one.

For instance, if we're narrowing all of humanity down to two options, I'd say that some of us are too stupid to know we're ignorant, and the rest of us are too ignorant to know we're stupid.

Sometimes, it's best to narrow it down to one option if you're looking to create camaraderie.

For instance, we are all turds polished in varying degrees. But we do have choices—we can choose to be one of the several varieties of turd that decidedly attempt to be the least shitty pieces of shit, or we can decide to be one of the many types that try to be the biggest pieces of shit imaginable.

The answer to an either/or can and should sometimes be neither/nor, especially when it's implied that you are undeniably some form of human defecation. On the contrary, if it's an either/or question regarding which type of cheese you'd like on your burger, the correct answer is simply, yes.

28. Future Revelations in Stupidity

11.9.21

Humility: There is a weird dichotomy between the ability to learn and confidence. Every day that I get a little less dumb, I become a little more aware of how dumb I was the day before and a little less confident that what I think today is not dumb. The inevitability of learning in the present is realizing the ignorance of your past.

Backstory and Inspiration: I know many educators who are open-minded, tactful, and mentally capable of adapting when presented with new information and ways of thought. That's how Darwin would have determined their value. When we are presented with new and more accurate information and choose to overlook it based on some misplaced sense of pride in the sometimes mistaken, sometimes short-sighted, sometimes purposely inaccurate, antiquated ways we were once taught, we fail ourselves–we fail our children.

Quality educators don't see this option as a possibility. Their conscience wouldn't allow it. Their passions are not based on unfounded egos. It would defy their goal.

The best are careful. The best change and regret the old, broken tools they were given to carry out their calling. The best see the advantages of an evolving curriculum. The best give your children the opportunity to make decisions and build their mindsets and preferences based on the most accurate, up-to-date, and unbiased information. I've known a few like this, and they can be found defending the hill of objectivity, empathy, compassion, and knowledge, however detrimental to our delicate, affected, subjective minds. We could all take a cue from their impassioned guidance.

I thought of the teachers struggling with the current climate of the educational system, as it is under the constant barrage of politicization and empowered ignorance, when I wrote this piece. I hope they will continue to fight for all of us despite the reluctance of the worst of us.

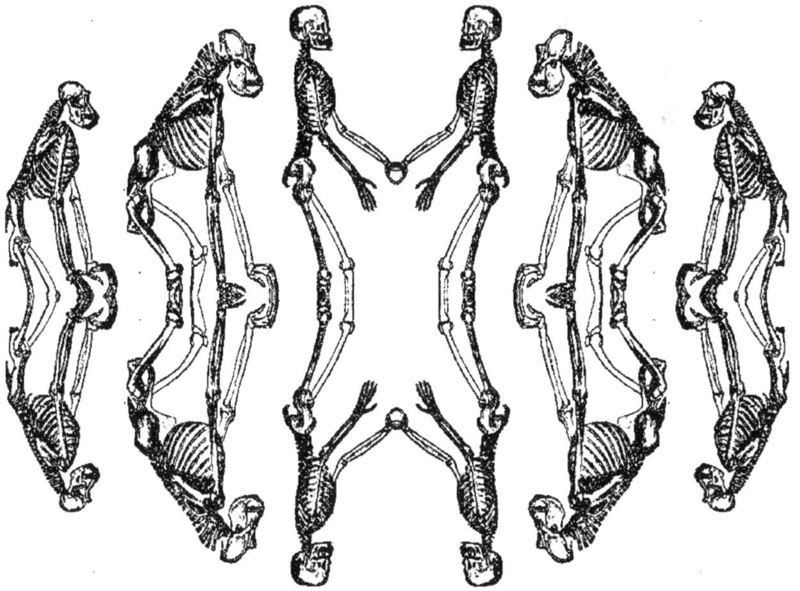

29. No Sleep Till Orbit City

11.16.21

Upholding antiquated, arbitrary tradition that serves no purpose is a waste of time, money, and resources. What qualifies as "serving a purpose" can be viewed as relative, I understand, but consider if the only value you're creating is satisfying your need to prevent change for the better because you fear it. Redefining what is important and useful is the only path to advancement. Digging in your heels for the simple fact of "This is the way we've always done it" is regressive and damaging. People who do these things are the reason we aren't living in Orbit City.

Jane! Get me off this crazy thing called…stupidity.

NO SLEEP TILL ORBIT CITY

30. The Odds of Afterlife

11.30.21

I view my thoughts on life, where it comes from, and the forever thereafter as if it were a small bet I made with money that I don't care if I lose–that I, for the most part, expect to lose. If we get to the end of it all, and I'm wrong, I'll be like, "Aw, man! Well played, life!" and I'll just go on about my business of being dead or whatever. If I'm right, I'll be like, "Ha! I knew it!" and I'll chuckle and go on about my business of being dead or whatever.

Leave some room for yourself to be wrong, so you won't hate yourself when you are…

and you will be…

at some point.

We all are.

31. Tragic Mirror on the Wall

12.21.21

The opposite of bad isn't worse.

If there's a bad universe in the mirror universe concept, we're it.

I recently read an article about scientists trying to open a door to a mirror universe. People commenting were concerned, but I don't think they should be. If the mirror universe is opposite us, that's the good side. They should be worried. I mean, what do you think is over there? Honest politicians who actually care about people? Ethical corporations? Quality, affordable healthcare? Justice? Equality?

There, the most exciting thing about getting a new phone is the 2U album that comes as a free option and can easily be deleted. There, the biggest news story is about *Ryle Kittenhouse bringing baked goods to an appreciation festival. Just watch out for **Reanu Keeves, that evil son of a bitch!

Don't worry about things that are different than what you've come to understand as "normal." There's a good chance that your "normal" is actually really shitty.

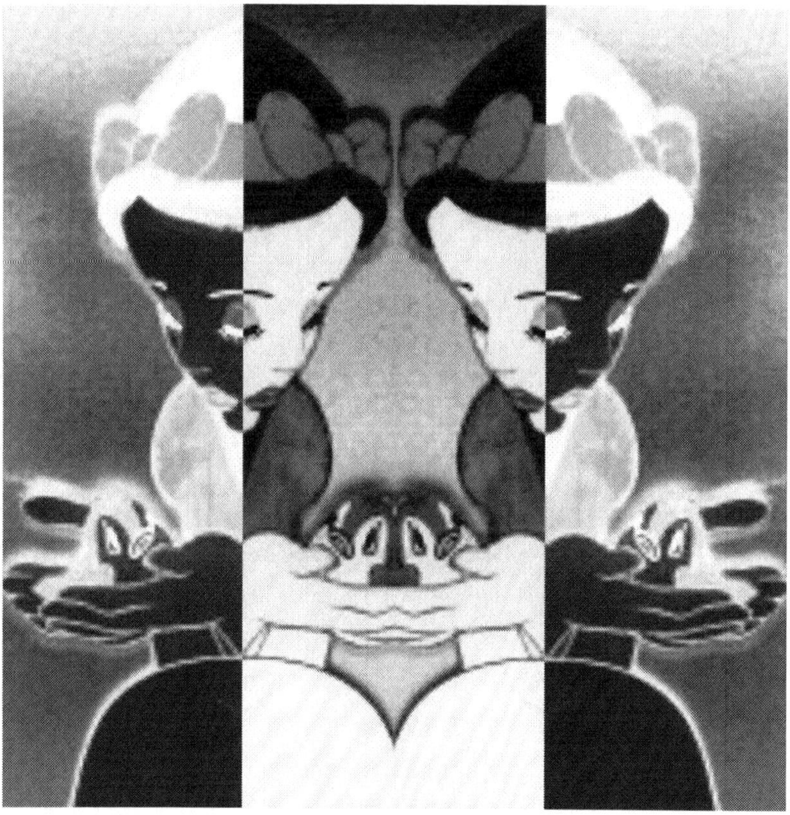

* **We, here at Thought & Other Absurdities, are aware of the fact that Ryle Kittenhouse and Reanu Keeves would not be true mirror-image spellings of these real-world names. So, we wanted to take a moment to address this. First and most obviously, these sound funnier. They are also much easier to pronounce. And, although we consider ourselves skeptics, we wanted to avoid any possible demon conjuring that trying to say any of this backward might trigger. Finally, and most importantly, if you want the names to be true mirror images, make up your own fucking mirror universe.

32. Dante's Infernal Paradise Lost and Found

12.28.21

Some of us (We) more readily accept pain over paradise because misery feels more like the reality that we believe—the reality that we have come to know—the reality that we deserve.

This is either the greatest lie of which we've ever convinced ourselves, or it is simply the hardest truth we've come to understand.

People want, so badly, to be understood that they sometimes wish the damage inflicted on them to be inflicted on everyone else, so they can feel that others truly empathize with them. Hence, the cliché, *Misery Loves Company*, but it's not entirely true. The real trick of it is that even when others have gone through something similar or subjectively worse, a person still won't believe the other individual because, while they want someone to understand them, they don't think it's possible. They feel their experience is so uniquely awful that no one else could've gone through it, or maybe they don't have the emotional availability to hurt for someone else because they are so deeply affected by their own situation.

Sometimes, it's simply because they don't feel that they deserve that kind of empathy. It becomes self-inflicted, and this is how a person isolates themselves from everyone they know and reality in general.

33. Market Pacifier

1.4.22

Our economic structure is designed to dictate the market, compelling companies to produce high-quality products to remain in business, lest their competitors develop something better, safer, longer-lasting, or more reliable, thereby capturing a larger market share and forcing subpar product-making businesses out of existence.

What actually happens—Companies compete for who can make the least expensive, passable product, using the guidelines of—"Can the average person afford this, understand this, does it play to the ignorant masses, will it last long enough but not so long that our future products don't sell, can we get away with it? What's the risk-to-reward ratio? Our market doesn't ensure that our consumables are better. Better, safer, healthier, more reliable, intelligent, these are luxury items. The standard model of everything is "profitable" and "marketable." These are the core values of the corporation of society.

We don't ask what the best quality product is. We ask what the best quality product is that I can afford. Luckily, there's enough advertising for most of it to convince enough of us that we are happy with what we can get, and we are pacified like babies with brand-name binkies.

34. Despite All the Rage

1.11.22

We destroy the world that created us, while the world we created destroys us. We have an anti-mutualistic relationship with reality.

It seems impossible, but we've been simultaneously convinced that we are rats in a corner, fighting for our lives, and lions who need to remind all else that we rule this reality. Our acts reflect that we believe both of these fallacies at the same time. We are no such things. We are deeply troubled humans with broken egos, confused and being taken advantage of.

"The world is a vampire."

-William Patrick Corgan

&

"We are the world."

-U.S.A for Africa

(basically every pop musician from the '80s)

They were all right.

35. Churchill Forgotten

1.25.22

Condemned to Repeat What Again?

Imagine you have amnesia and can't remember a single historical event. You have to make all of your decisions without any knowledge of what may or may not have happened in similar situations in the past. There is no context. Every situation is subject to mistakes that have already been made. Now you know how it feels to be an average human being in the 2020s.

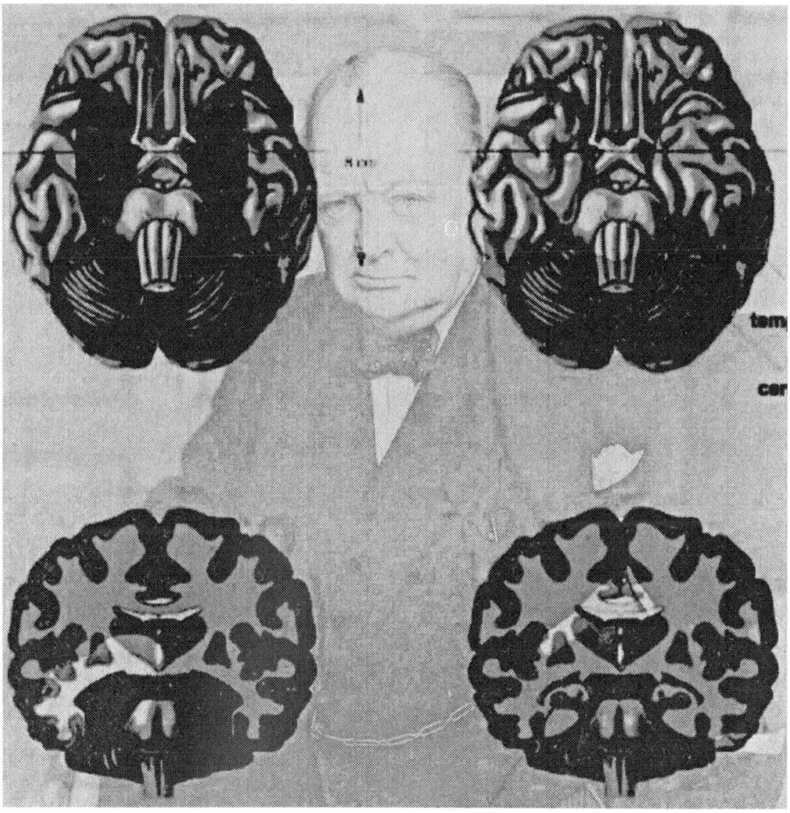

36. Finite Parallels

2.1.22

I think we are already living, simultaneously, in parallel universes. There's the you that you used to be, the you that you are now, the parent you, the online you, the work you, the you when you're alone, the you when you're with friends, and no matter how much you are yourself in any of these situations, they are still all very distinct people. The difficulty of being alive is figuring out which one of these variations or what combination of them is actually you and trying not to lose sight of that in the face of being pulled in each of those thousands of directions all at the same time.

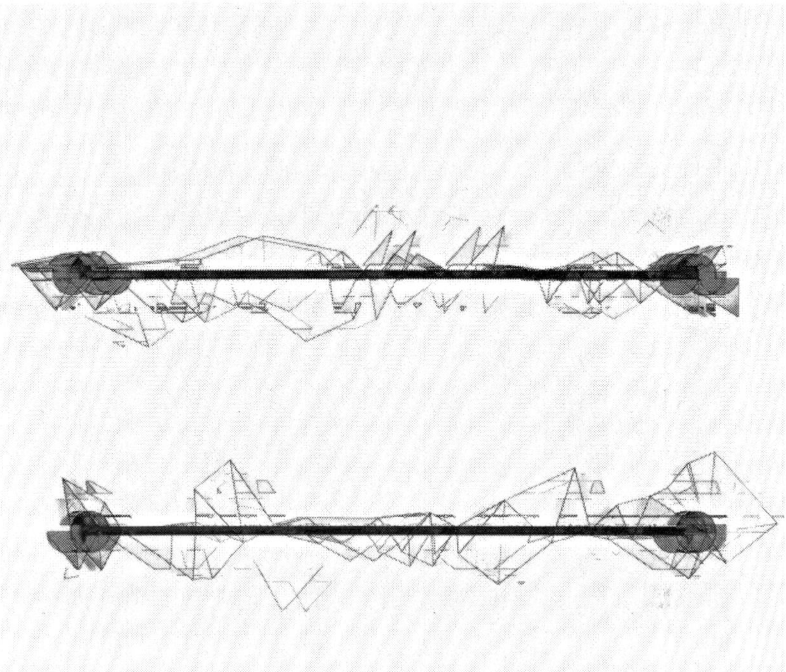

37. Deep State Hypnosis

2.8.22

I think we're all going to feel a little silly about all of this bickering and arguing when we wake up and find out that it's 1997, and the past twenty-five years were just a hypnotic dream state due to subliminal messages that Bill Clinton had covert governmental agencies add to the aptly named Hypnotize song by The Notorious B.I.G. in an effort to suppress outrage over the Monica Lewinski situation. This also explains the untimely demise of Biggie Smalls, AKA Big Poppa. Operation Deep State Hypnosis was designed to give us decades of reasons and dire world circumstances to desensitize us to any wrongdoings of the current administration, and, so far, has been an astounding success.

Hey, if everyone else is allowed to make up wild conspiracy theories, so can I.

38. Judge, Jury, and Protozoan Parasite

2.15.22

One-third of the population is infected with a protozoan parasite found largely in domesticated cats. The parasite causes its host to lose intelligent fear for legitimate threats to its well-being.

I guess that explains the popularity of the *No Fear* brand t-shirts in the early '90s

It's just lovely that we live in a time when we view everything as a challenge to our individuality, intelligence, and freedom, as if we feel like we are being dared to do something against our will. We're like stubborn toddlers in a morning power struggle to not wear our pants. It's like, c'mon, assholes! Can't we just wash our hands? No one is going to think you any less of an individual for having proper hygiene.

When it feels like we're being judged, we might do better to just consider that it may just be that people are actually rooting for us, hoping we'll make rational decisions for our well-being. Perhaps it's just everyone wanting to believe we're not complete idiots, and we're just making it difficult for anyone else to believe anything else.

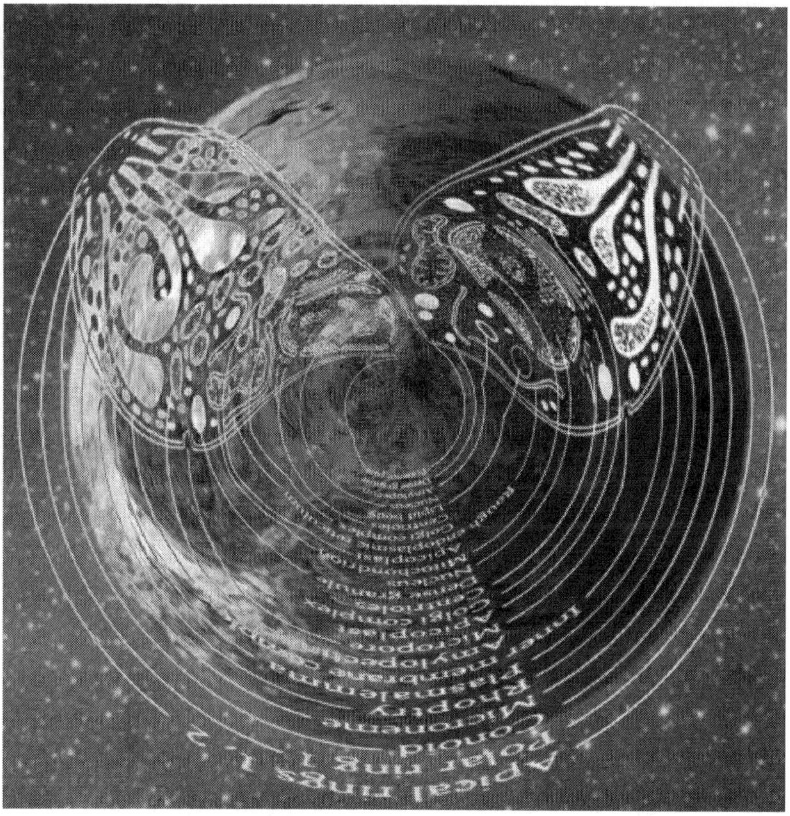
Apical rings 1 - 2
Polar ring 1
Conoid
Microneme
Rhoptry
Plasmalemma

39. Goldfish Arsonists from the Future

2.22.22

Recently, scientists taught a goldfish to drive. Seriously, look it up. Like we couldn't find anything else for our scientists to be working on? This is what we're doing? This is the reason people from the future don't trust us with time travel.

I always love it when humanity lives up to its true potential. Sometimes, it's as if we're actively trying to get whatever created us and any possible extraterrestrial life to hate us. Maybe there is a silver lining, though. Who knows, maybe this research will lead to a scientific breakthrough in figuring out a way to teach people how to drive.

Have we ever considered that maybe we haven't met time travelers from the future because there isn't a future? If the present is any indication, I don't think it's entirely out of the question to speculate that maybe we don't last long enough to figure it out.

Some people discount the possibility of time travel by saying, "Well, if it's possible in the distant future, don't you think we would have met time travelers by now?" I don't think that disputes time travel in the least. Another option may be that we have met time travelers. Maybe they're just smart enough not to tell us about it. It's my guess that if there are time-traveling visitors from the future, they're not sharing the secrets of time travel with us because they don't want us to go to the future and fuck it up worse than we already did.

It would be like giving an arsonist a can of gas and directions to your house.

40. Take Me Off, Take Off Me

3.8.22

Some people have completely detached themselves from reality, and it fascinates me.

I find it interesting that we see disconnecting from reality as any sort of respite or solution when one of our biggest problems is that so many of us are, in fact, wildly disconnected from reality. I wonder if escaping it is really of any benefit. Is it possible that some of this stress is self-inflicted? Maybe some of us are trying to worry enough to make up for all of those who we feel aren't worrying enough or at all. Unfortunately, that's not really possible, and worrying for ourselves is probably already more than many of us are even capable of at this point.

41. Kiss My New Butt

3.17.22

We are living in a renaissance of stupidity.

An educator was recently fired for reading a children's book to, get this, children.

A book, mind you, that makes kids comfortable talking about their insecurities to the end of realizing we all have them, while also being fun enough to get children interested in reading. Clearly, this type of madness and debauchery must be stopped. Add this to the long list of unanswerable questions ending with, "what in the actual fuck?"

What I'm really hearing from all of this is that droves of adults are openly admitting that they are incapable of comprehending the meaning behind books written for children. So brave!

Read them and understand them before you ban them.

If you need a new butt like the child in the story, I imagine the head of the person who got this educator fired would be a perfectly sufficient and mostly unnoticeable replacement.

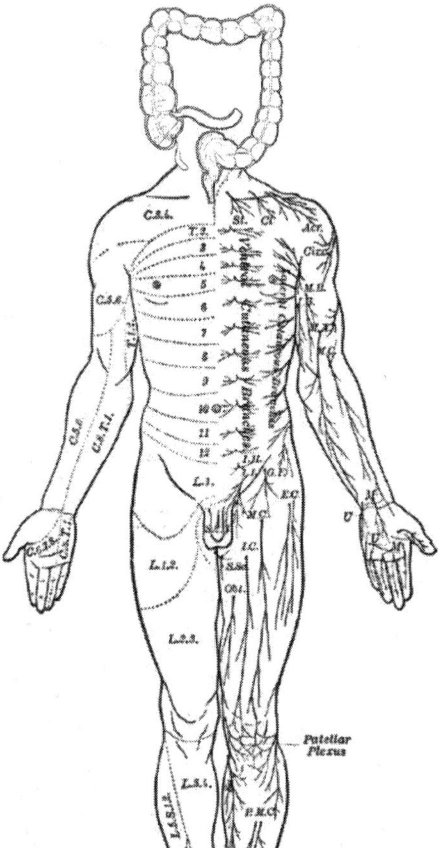
Patellar
Plexus
Sun

42. The Ethics of Blasphemy (Jeu on Paper Part III)

3.22.22

"It's perfectly legal" is the hallmark statement of someone who is doing something devoid of morals and ethics. Policy follows money cloaked in false faith. A befitting punishment—an end-all in the question of whether or not life is "fair" would be these individuals being punished for their sins in the exact ways that they pretend to believe.

What is acceptable, fair, right, and just is no longer dictated by morality, decency, law, constitution, or religion. Maybe it never was. These notions are dictated by money, the market, and popularity. People, politicians, shareholders—they'll pretend that morality, decency, law, constitution, and religion played a crucial role in their decision-making when, and only when, they stand to profit more from doing so.

Welcome to another heretical economy. It's not the first. We can only hope it is the last.

43. Night Owl in the Apple Tree

3.29.22

Children are evil geniuses.

Our five-year-old takes inventory of everything we ask her to do that she refuses to do all day long. When it's bed-time, she asks to do everything we begged her to do, but she wouldn't do, knowing that we are more likely to say yes to something she knows we want her to do so that she can stay up a little longer. Water, healthy snacks, more reading, etc. "Remember? You said I needed to drink more water, right? You said I should eat apples." It's diabolical! All day, these items were arguments while she pushed our buttons and every boundary, and did absolutely everything she knows for certain that she is not supposed to do. But it's a setup. At night, she flips the script and suddenly wants to do every single thing we asked her to do the entire day. It's brilliant, and it's eleven pm, and we're eating enough apples and drinking enough water to be healthy for the next eighty years or so.

Sleep tight.

44. idGnorance (Freudian Slap Part II)

4.8.22

We ought to be more unlike the things we find appalling, but such is rarely the case.

Our ego used to be the arbiter between our morality, or conscience, and our instinct. We have little morality left, very little conscience, and though our instincts are for shit, they're now running the show.

Use the same words that you would normally use to defend yourself, your ideas, and your preferences to figure out a way to extend to others the courtesy and understanding you offer yourself. The self-created difficulty of transferring this type of compassion is where all of this is falling apart. We regress into the ignorant id.

Welcome to Uncivilization.

Your ego is
far from super!

45. Reflections in Populism

4.26.22

We are hellbent on justifying our own flaws and guilty consciences with the actions of others. We do this to the point of convincing even ourselves that we support and believe in the unspeakable acts of the obviously depraved. We defend them as if we are defending ourselves. We want the world to condone what they've done so that we can feel that the things we think and do are acceptable. We fly the flags of devils in defense of our demons. The things for which we hate ourselves the most determine for whom we are willing to fight. Our poorly behaved celebrities and politicians—our infamous yet idolized criminals are only funhouse mirrors in which we see ourselves. If this seems like an exaggeration, see if you can recall yourself or anyone else defending someone with, "I would have done the same thing."

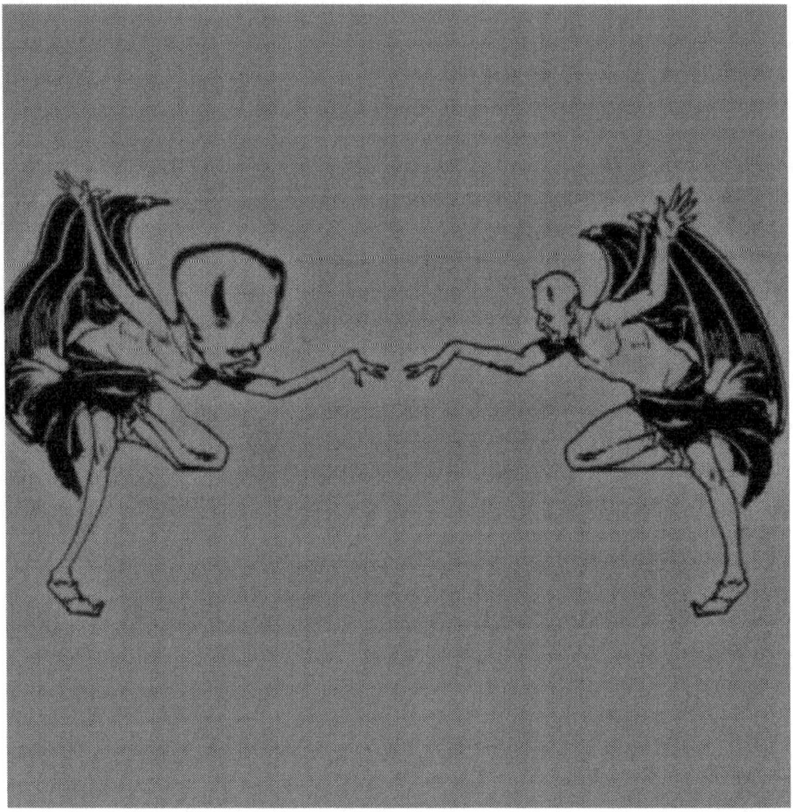

46. Ants Under a Magnifying Glass

5.17.22

"Do bugs have school?" my five-year-old daughter asked me.

"No, they don't have school, baby," I responded in a robotic and classically trained human way. Then I thought about it because I don't just want to pass on my conditioned understanding or misunderstanding of the world. And, like anything else, the more you consider all possibilities, the less clear any sort of answer becomes. What if they fucking do? I don't really know. In our perception, bugs don't have school, but maybe our perception isn't reality to a bug. We think we know, but the more we learn, the more we come to understand how little we know. We become increasingly aware of our ignorance with each passing moment. We only overthink things like this until we realize how little thought we've actually given to them. I don't want to confuse her, but my guess is that no matter how I responded, she wouldn't be any more confused than the rest of us.

Next time, maybe I'll say, "You know what, Sweetie? People don't think bugs have school, but people are pretty dumb, so who knows."

47. The Reality of Perception

5.24.22

Since each of our perceptions is our own reality, reality is created by our perceptions. This makes each of us the creators of our own divergent universes. These realities run parallel with some universes, while they cross and overlap with others. We cross dimensions most with those whom we consider friends and family, and we begin to consider the nature of their universes, which forever alters our own.

ORTH
OCEAN
UNITED STATES

48. Viral Humanity

6.7.22

We are things not unlike those studied in Petri dishes, save for the fact that they may be operating on a purely biologically instinctual level, whereas we choose to be many of the things–ways we are. It's as if our prevailing drive is to infect every other person with our personal experience-distorted ideas, opinions, and values. Can't we just live and let leave everybody the fuck alone?

The worst diseases imaginable are transmitted through words.

Why is it always the most insanely boring people who seem to want everyone in the world to be exactly like them? Watch The Walking Dead and imagine if it were just zombies. No matter your opinion of the show, I think we can all agree that an hour of watching only the zombies walk around would be a lot more like standing in line at the DMV. So, why are so many of us trying so desperately to turn everyone else into our boring selves as if we have no idea of how much more mundane and terrible life would be if every person were the same?

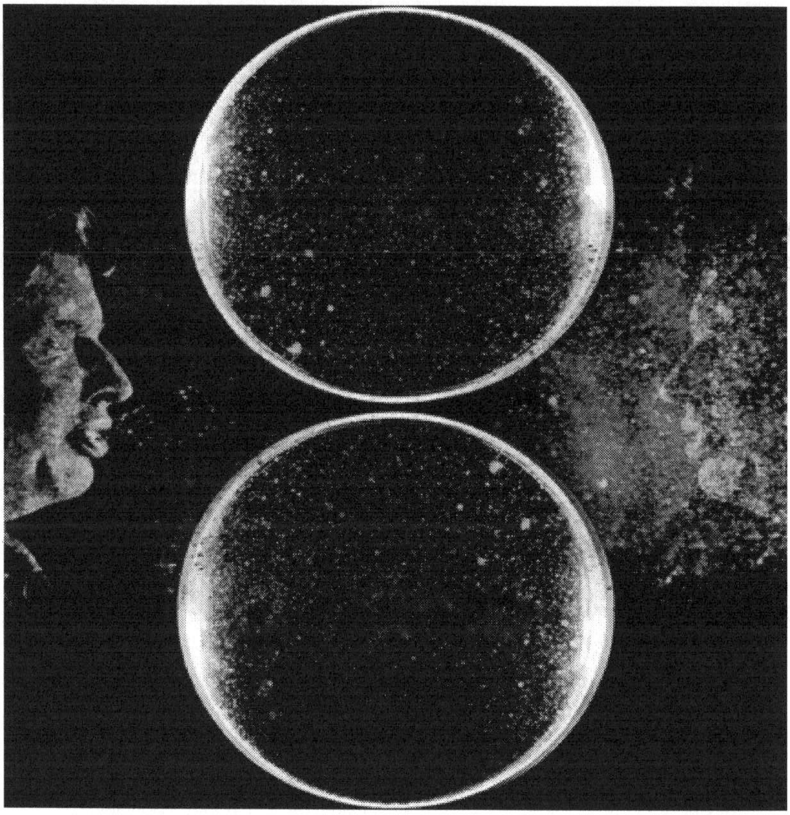

49. The Happily Unconverted

6.14.22

Aside from those actions which purposely cause others pain and anguish, I not only tolerate your preferences, I fully support them…FOR YOU! I'm rarely interested in being evangelized or doing so to someone else. I'll speak/write my mind, sure, and if it just so happens to change someone's opinion, fabulous. If not, cool. And I'm interested in the way you think and the way you form your opinions. I'm listening. I'm paying attention. If it strikes me, I'll join your cause and make it ours. Sometimes, though, your cause is not and will never be mine. We all need to find a way to respect that.

50. Flight of the Platypus

6.8.22

As humans, we spend a lot of time looking at other people, creatures, and ideas not our own, and we think, Oh, well, that's weird. Think about your own body—how it works. Think about where your ideas even come from. Think about your thoughts. Think about how we think about the nature of our existence and how, to the best of our often failed and highly suspect knowledge, we're one of, if not the only species that even considers any of this (though I seriously doubt that's true). Now, that's fucking weird. We should all just be happy to be weirdos and applaud other creatures and people and their ideas for their weirdness. In summation, everything is weird, and so, nothing is weird.

51. Typing Into the Void

7.20.22

The most difficult thing about writing, art, and really, life, in general, is that our dreadful human minds don't allow us to truly believe anyone who says that we're good at it or that we're terrible at it, so you really need to be doing it for yourself.

Underwood

52. Poop and Turdcumstance

8.9.22

We're all victims of circumstance beyond our control now. The only thing that we can do to salvage some sort of decent existence is to find something–anything to be happy about and roll around in it like my dog does when he finds a turd in the yard that he likes. Get the stink of the things you enjoy all over yourselves and let everyone smell it, and if they like it, let them join in because they're your people. Vonnegut referred to it as your karass. I don't bring this up because karass has the word ass in it, and I've clearly gone way too far with this fecal simile, but (and it took a lot for me not to spell that with an extra *t*) rather because of the meaning of this word that he created, which is a group of individuals who are somehow linked spiritually. Or, maybe you're a karass of one, and that's fine too, as long as you're still rolling around on your happy turd.

53. We, Robot

8.16.22

Is Automation Ruling the Nation?

If you're worried about how it's going to be when robots take all of our jobs, don't. It already happened. Call any customer service line and see if you feel like you're speaking to an actual human being with empathy who's not programmed to a mindless script from which they cannot stray. We're all robots already.

The day will come when we need do nothing. It will be our choice to enrich our own lives with self-fulfilling endeavors or slumber under the alluring blanket of boundless consumerism to the end of doing only more nothing.

54. Diet Justice

8.24.22

Thoughts on the "Supreme" and the Supremely Corrupt

In truth, it was a callow, pathetic passing of responsibility, so that those who stood to lose votes for their party by making an actual decision wouldn't have to be accountable for the outcome. Regardless of where you stand on the matter, it was a weak shift of a once, rightfully or wrongfully, assumed responsibility by sad, agenda-obsessed, money and power-grubbing dirtbags. It's all so much worse and more disgusting than we may fully realize in our initial gut reactions. It was a practice in false neutrality, risk assessment, and mitigation of loss of power, money, control, election seats, and the padded and privileged lap of golden luxury in which our elected officials are shamefully showered. Diet Justice–now with all the power and none of the accountability.

Diet Justice
All the Power - Zero Accountability

55. Way Fairer

8.30.22

Those who say, "Well, life isn't fair," are the people most concerned with everyone else suffering the way they have, so that life is fair to them.

Maybe we should spend more time validating people who think most everything in life is now kind of bullshit. Every day, we endure cliché horseshit like "Buck up, Buttercup" and "No one said life would be easy." I'm going the opposite direction. Shit sucks, and people are justified and have a right to be annoyed and disappointed. If your soul-sucking mottos like "Life is what you make it" are true, just know that they make life pretty shitty for people who are angry for legitimate reasons, of which there are many.

Life isn't fair. Sure. But that doesn't mean you should do everything in your power to ensure it stays that way.

Let's try not to keep things status quo if the status quo is bullshit. Let's change the bullshit and start a new status quo.

56. Hokum's Razor

9.27.22

People love, fear, and are generally enamored by things they believe to be different, otherworldly, or voodoo. We are so arrogant as a species that when we witness something we can't immediately explain, we think some magical, mystical force must be at play because it certainly can't be that our brilliant, all-knowing minds couldn't figure it out if it weren't. And so, we make up some crazy shit that's most likely even less believable than the truth. There's a light in the sky. Of course, I can explain it. There's a giant, all-knowing being who put it there.

Sometimes, these ideas take root and evolve and are somehow embraced by hordes of people because it's more convenient to be given answers than it is to figure out life. Most of the greatest tragedies in our history happened because of someone coming up with a bullshit reason for something they didn't understand or for which they didn't want to be held, in any way, accountable. A woman doesn't want to be beaten with a stick as thick as a thumb, have fourteen babies, and have her entire life decided by a man or some supposed ethereal force. Well…she must be a witch. It works its way into everything. There are economic troubles…must be immigrants or a political party that disagrees with my chosen political affiliation. There must be an enemy. Maybe it's people whose faith is in opposition to mine–people who've been indoctrinated into something different from what I've been indoctrinated into. They must be converted or eradicated for the sanctity of life, as I feel it should be—as I was told it should be. From gods and witches to populist politicians, we've allowed ourselves to be convinced that our greatest atrocities are justified until the judgment of time proves otherwise, and often, even after that.

My made-up stuff is better than your made-up stuff. Let's destroy everything to decide who's right.

57. The Sandwich Murders

1.11.23

Have you ever watched someone do something that should be completely routine, but they somehow manage to defy all basic and accepted processes as if the fundamental, everyday task was some bizarre thing they'd never witnessed, as if they'd been asked to turn themselves inside out, as if they'd been asked to hammer a nail with a glob of gelatin?

A few days ago, I watched someone try to make me a sandwich at a deli. They were as barbaric and clumsy as a thousand-pound grizzly bear whose hands had fallen asleep. I watched them pulverize meat, veggies, and bread into an abomination of mangled ingredients resembling something that had accidentally fallen into a garbage disposal. It was almost as difficult to watch as it was to try to look away. When I was finally able to turn my head from the criminal disaster, my eyes met with the other sandwich hopefuls waiting for their lunch to be abused in front of them, their eyes wrought with horror and confusion.

I can't stop thinking about it—this culinary desecration. How does any person, let alone one whose particular job is to do so, fuck up making a simple sandwich? I thought about how this might affect the rest of their life. I felt a deep sense of concern for their partner's genitalia. I hoped they'd never need to get something out of their eye with those mauling, clearly knuckle-less hammer-paws. Could it have been on purpose? Had I angered this sandwich-murdering stranger? What manner of damage must they self-inflict while wiping their ass? Imagine the rectal bruising! I may need to speak to a psychiatrist. It has deeply affected me.

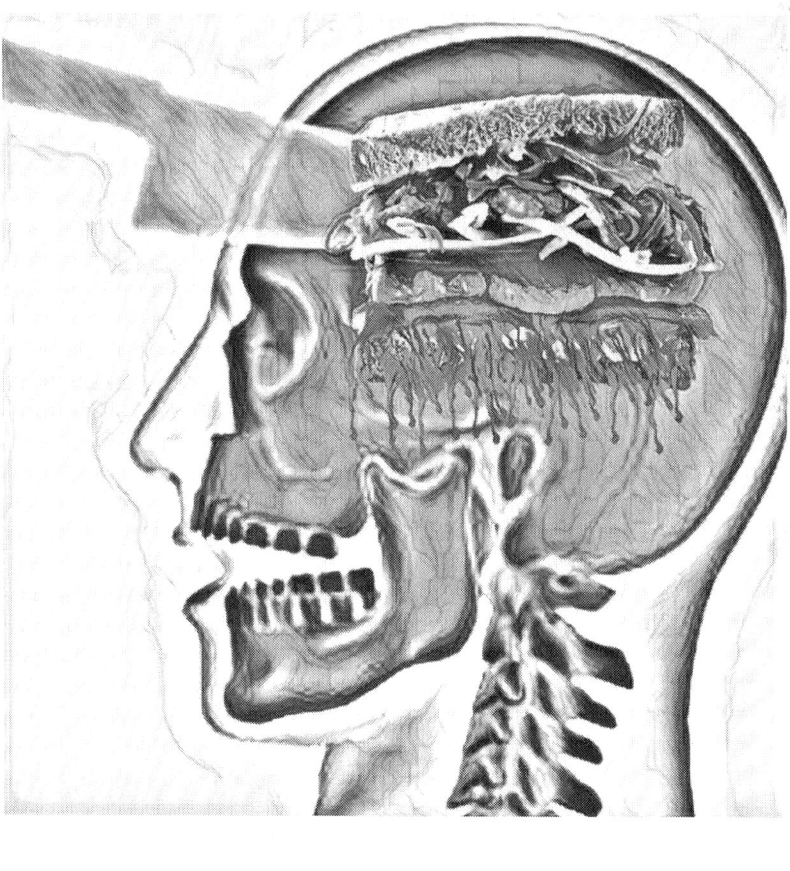

58. The Patron Saints of Patronization

2.16.23

It always strikes me how people can put a bunch of innocuous, perfectly fine words together and make them mean something so ugly.

This or that, either/or—false dichotomies of one or the other. Sometimes, it's neither. Often, it's both.

In this particular case, it's the latter.

I listened to the sanctimonious verbal sewage philosophies of a profoundly misguided yet widely celebrated pop culture sophist. They spat logical-sounding fallacies about their belief in the limited existence of two options for internalizing our feelings about people and the descendants of people who have been and are still victimized in some of the greatest atrocities humanity (term being used loosely here) has ever committed against humanity (and more appropriately here).

As a definite, they stated that we can either feel sympathy for the people who are or have been or whose ancestors have been oppressed and murdered due to their heritage and beliefs, or we can admire them for their perseverance.

As if the range of human emotion were limited to feeling only one thing at a time.

This is almost always a lie, and it is generally directed at making us think and behave in the way the perpetrator of the lie wants us to think and behave. It is rarely for any purpose other than some confused and misinformed belief that there is some personal gain to be had from it, though there never truly is.

We can mourn a people's incalculable losses while also being amazed at their inconceivable strength.

We can feel these things simultaneously.

We are not confined to this or that, one or the other.

And, even in modern times, with some of these horrendous decimations of cultures and oppressions of swaths of human life behind us, we should appreciate the harrowing difficulties of people who know these are their pasts—people who are aware that their fellow humans had to find some additional, how-does-this-affect-me reason to help stop these horrors, and yet, against all logic and reason, don't absolutely detest every other kind of people.

It is beyond our embarrassingly beloved demagogues' realm of understanding.

Beyond their privileged and pathetic pseudo-logic, and clearly well beyond their capacity for empathy, compassion, and kindness.

They have found our weakest's weaknesses, and they have exploited them.

They sit on a mountain of millions of reasons made of green linen and precious metals that we gave them for telling us the absolving untruths we so desperately want to hear.

Behold,

The Patron Saints of Patronization.

ELMO'S FIRE

59. The Mount Rushmore of Four Horsemen

4.24.23

Self-Deprecation, Depreciation, and Decapitation

Humans need three things to survive: Water, Food, and Air. Humanity needs three more: Wherewithal, Forethought, and Compassion. We've poisoned each of these things in the pursuit of wealth.

The more we cut corners, ignore the human condition, pretend needs are commodities, and loosen oversight on profits, the more we will see of these preventable tragedies, the more damned, sicker, and weaker we will become, the less human, the more our hubris will fill the mass grave we call civilization. We are Conquest in our trivial pursuit of power and profit. We are Famine in the condoning of hunger with plentiful resources and complicit in the tainting of our nourishment. We are War in our hearts, in our minds, and in our streets. In all of these and in every way, we are Death. We personify our own demise. This is what it means when people talk about stupidity being the fall of humankind. This is the way the world ends, not with a bang, but a whimper. And we may not be heading for the end of life in the strictest of terms, but it does seem that we're sliding down an ever-steepening slope toward the end of life, at the very least, as we know it–a life worth living for a majority of us. If you're someone who mostly believes, as I do, that life is better than the alternative, I would advocate for you to engage with someone who doesn't see it as such and allow them to enlighten you as to why so that you might find the depth of compassion that will undoubtedly be required of all of us should we have any hope of clawing our way back up that steep slope.

60. Rancor the Anchor

5.4.23

At some point in the recent past, some of us began blaming our problems on progress instead of adapting and moving forward. Due to our discomfort with change and mental inability to accept the fault or blame that might allow for growth, some of us gnawed at the hands of natural, societal evolution. It's a repeating pattern. While some take two steps forward, others argue that it's regression and grasp for the reins to pull all of us a step and a half back in the wrong direction until the will and numbers of those with this mindset fade. Then a new set of detractors takes their place, allowing us to regain that step and a half, only to become the same inhibitors for the next steps. I only wonder what we could achieve and the speed at which we could achieve it, without this inherent inclination to perpetually fight the momentum of growth.

61. The Shape of Change

5.16.23

I think we may be better off if we could stop being so convinced that the way we believe things have "always been" is the way things actually are or should be. Discovery itself isn't change. Just because we didn't understand something in the past, that doesn't make it new. With discovery, our thinking needs to shift with the best possible evidence available. We should be thrilled when we find out we were wrong about something. That generally means we're coming closer to understanding something.

Our biological makeup didn't dramatically evolve overnight. Gender didn't inexplicably mutate in the past few years. The Earth didn't suddenly undergo some epic transformation when it went from flat to spherical in the eyes of common knowledge. Our understanding of these things changed. For the duration of our lifetimes, they are as they were and will remain for the most part. We just know more about them now. Do we have a perfect understanding of everything? Absolutely not, but with each passing day, we come closer to that seemingly, if not entirely, unachievable goal.

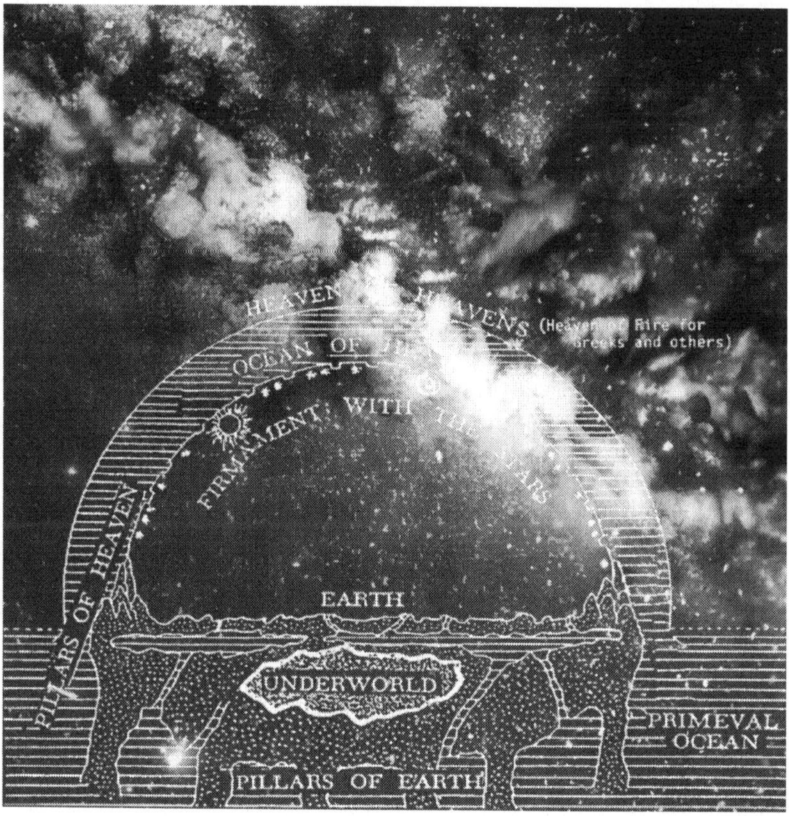
HEAVEN
HEAVENS
and others)
OCEAN OF
FIRMAMENT WITH
PILLARS OF HEAVEN
EARTH
UNDERWORLD
PRIMEVAL OCEAN
PILLARS OF EARTH

62. Culture by Gaslight

6.8.23

The term gaslighting is probably well overused at this point, but I do feel as though we're all being gaslit–gaslighted, or however we're saying it as a past participle, by culture–a culture we've created. I would personally like to thank society for making life as miserable as possible, while also asserting that if we aren't able to figure out a way to be happy despite the conditions, it's our own fault because there's something wrong with us. I imagine this is how many of us feel, rushing here and there to places we don't want to be to do things we don't want to do for a "living" with which we aren't remotely satisfied, instead of spending time doing things we love with people we care about. All while being harangued by preposterous claims of how we can simply change it all with some "#positivevibes." It's a fucking real shit sandwich we've cooked up for ourselves, isn't it?

63. The Definition Indefinite

6.13.23

I don't think it's absurd to consider that maybe our hardline definitions of male and female are precisely the cause of people feeling that they don't belong to either category. Honestly, given the current state of humanity and our perceptions of one another, who would even want to be considered a person at all at this point?

One thing more powerful than our ability to convince ourselves that we understand is our ignorance of that which we believe to understand. Will we ever stop using definite terms to describe indefinite things?

64. Junkies for Capitalism

6.20.23

(A CaffeiNation)

I dislike how we use cute little words and sayings to describe how miserable life is, like "adulting" and "TGIF," or the "work hard/play hard" mentality. We need to stop patronizing ourselves. How about we just make life more fucking bearable and give people as much time to relax and enjoy being alive as we spend torturing ourselves to keep this fucked-up machine running.

-From a previous social media post of mine, but I thought it applied nicely here.

...

For all of this to work, a pretty good percentage of us have to wake up well before we're naturally inclined to do so, and we have to go and do something we'd probably prefer not to do so that the wheels of our society keep slowly grinding on, despite our misery.

And just how could anyone or anything possibly get most of us to do this without drugs and brainwashing? Well, you don't do it without drugs and brainwashing. Those are precisely the tactics needed to give the masses some unity of direction. So, we employ the two most powerful tools of motivation–a false sense of pride for enduring hardships and a Starbucks on every corner.

You see, pride and caffeine addictions are the two most significant driving forces of our society. These aren't the only tools. There are also nicotine, which plays a less crucial role now that we've been begrudgingly told how horrible it is for us, and alcohol, which, in an odd way, keeps us just as productive as caffeine.

We wake in the morning and supercharge our brains and bodies so we can go and do these things we'd probably prefer not to be doing. When we need to wind down from this false energy and forget about doing that thing we'd probably prefer not to be doing, we have a few drinks to unwind, unnaturally slowing our bodies and thoughts so that we can rest or, at least, feel some disconnection from the trials of our days. Meanwhile, this entire time, we're injected with this rhetoric that convinces us that all of this is, somehow, impressive–something to boast about.

We start our day with uppers. We end our day with downers, and we're so bamboozled by these things and the notion that we've done something important that we believe we love them—that we enjoy them—that they're fun. We make silly jokes about them and have dumb sayings like, "Don't talk to me before my coffee," or "I could really use a drink." But what we really should be doing—what we could really use, is a grande go-the-fuck-back-to-bed-until-we're-rested with an extra pump of that-bullshit-can-wait.

We don't love coffee—we're addicted to caffeine.

We don't like alcohol—we desperately need a quick and easy way to relax and distract our brains from the insane tension that this life creates.

Of course, there are healthy alternatives…if we have more time, more energy, more money, and less of a need to do things we'd prefer not to do, but it's a hell of a lot more convenient to fix our problems with magical elixirs.

I'm not condemning anyone who enjoys or partakes in these things. I'm just as enamored with them as anyone else.

We are all addicts.

We are all damned.

65. America's Value Menu

7.12.23

It's getting more expensive every day, but it's just as terrible for you as it ever was.

We should probably start looking at curing society's ills from the same perspective that we view the progression of what we refer to as modern medicine. I think and write about this a lot. I imagine it seems very plain and obvious to so many of us, and yet it still has no effect on a large portion of humanity's need to uphold tradition. Our religions, our laws, our social norms, they're all based on the needs of the time in which they were established. People want so badly to cement themselves in something they can count on—some sort of constant, and we get overwhelmed by the reality that these things need constant care, constant amendment, constant evolution to apply to the present.

If America had "values," and those "values" were "righteous," how did we end up here? Seems to me that the "values" people so fondly remember are, in fact, responsible for the current state of affairs. Perhaps, despite their intent, which may have at one time seemed "right" and "good," they are now simply wrong and obsolete, like so many ancient medical practices. Maybe it's not these old ideas we need, but new and better ideas, so we aren't bloodletting to cure our societal ills.

66. The Post-Dollar-Store-Apocalypse

4.16.24

The year is 2030. There are no more homes, and only two businesses remain. Nearly every structure has been converted into a Dollar Store. People sleep in hostel-style bunks in the stockrooms next to the back-stock inventory. Nearly expired Cheetos, discontinued candy bars, RC Cola, and the like are the only forms of sustenance.

Everyone dreams of making it to the store manager position and saving enough singles to move into a fancy neighborhood where they can live in a closet at a Five Below, the only other retail store in existence. But that reality is merely a fever dream for most, and that's if it even actually exists.

City, state, and national government entities are no more. Strict order is kept by The Supreme Being–a network of self-checkout registers with a single, sentient, artificially intelligent consciousness. We exist only for its amusement, forced to perform improv comedy using items from the shelves or be blinded by barcode scanning lasers.

Despite the meager conditions, very few attempt

revolt. Most claim contentment, citing the generosity of the Self-Checkout Register deity, as it provides all the nourishment necessary for life via highly processed snack chips and sodas.

DOLLAR GENERALCIDE

67. Hard Work Hardly Working

5.14.24

Hard work only begets harder work.

Good fortune and privilege are rewarded with greater fortune and further privilege.

If you are unlucky, do the least amount of work possible. There is still a chance you may get lucky, but luck has never been given in trade for our most harrowing labors, and you will be no more likely to have good fortune and privilege for exhausting yourself into the dirt. Any attempt to dissuade you from this notion comes from a place of inherited beliefs or manipulation in order for someone else to benefit from your labors.

Instead, utilize your short existence inventing ways to enjoy it. Maybe hard work is enjoyment for some. For some, finding this enjoyment may be the hardest work of all.

68. Let Me Inertain You

5.21.24

So far as I've been able to discern, we're only really here to try to entertain ourselves until we're no longer here.

It also occurs to me that anything we busy ourselves with that doesn't help us achieve that goal is a distraction meant to confuse us into believing otherwise—that there is some greater meaning. This notion makes all of us believe, in some part, that enjoyment is frivolous—something meant to pass the time between laboring and making a "valid" contribution to society. Even those who desperately attempt not to buy into it bear the guilt of generations of beleaguered souls haunting us with antiquated notions that were never right—shamed for the imaginary slight of our hedonistic nature by the omnipotent inventions of our imaginations turned into what we can only believe to be the voices of our conscience. Mind you, not for the grandest of indiscretions, which might contribute to the detriment of others, but rather the simple pleasures of life that disrupt the flow of hardship being passed downward, which allows for the silken cream of prosperity and contentment to be pushed to the top. In turn, those who bring the most joy of entertainment are held in high regard, but because we cannot fully accept this simplistic principle, and we love to confuse ourselves that there must be more to it, those who bring the most misery are also deemed important and regarded as leaders—religious, political, or industry—who do the hard, serious, "important" work of causing the greatest harm. For what? I've never been able to fathom an answer to this question. For everything we've done—every decision that brought us to this point—every tired cliché that prods us like cattle to serve a "greater" purpose, I am not entertained.

Find a way to enjoy some small part of this life without being a dick to other people.

69. Undo You: Part 2

6.11.24

Sure, bad things are happening, but you can't let it affect you.

It's absurd that anyone champions this line of logic.

Instead, maybe allow it to affect you. Allow your compassion and empathy for those who are experiencing "bad things" to guide your personal choices and decisions, rather than always focusing on yourself. If you're wondering what's wrong with the world, it's that everybody decided they don't like feeling bad about things, so they pretend they don't fucking exist. And guess how much attention and consideration problems that don't exist get.

I know the bullshit response will be, *but everything we do is selfish.* Yeah, sure, but why not make other people's struggles part of your own? That way, even when you're doing selfish things, they still benefit more than just you. It's called caring, and that's what we purposely choose not to do.

UN•DO YOU

/U(H)N DEW U/

IDIOM • MAINLY MY IRRITATED PSYCHE • INFORMAL

1. A CALL FOR OTHERS TO UNF[CENSORED]K THEMSELVES IN RESPONSE TO THE PHRASE *YOU DO YOU*

FROM MY MENTAL DICTIONARY

70. Aye, AI!

8.1.24

People aren't actually afraid of robotics and AI doing our work for us and taking our jobs. What we're honestly and rightfully frightened of is that some people are so evil that they would use it to their personal benefit while letting everyone else have nothing, including the means by which to gain something…anything. Somewhere in the back of our minds, we remember watching Scooby Doo, and we realize people are the real monsters. What we truly fear is that work is our only bargaining chip with the ruling class, and once it's gone, there'll be no reason for us. It's a pretty good indicator that things were already swirling down the drain long before technology could make it scary.

71. Ever the Two Shall Meet

8.13.24

We are living in distinctly opposing realities of perception. While most of us are experiencing a dystopian hellscape or purgatory at best, some of us are basking in the warm light of a glorious utopia. When the former hear the words of the latter, they seem impossibly disconnected from the only reality of which the former are aware. The same disbelief is found in the opposing direction. These are the simultaneously existing, separate realities of seemingly parallel universes, though it is one for all in all but our perceptions, where the two are destined never to intersect. They always do, though, when we are all made meat to feed the insatiably ravenous teeth and guts of life.

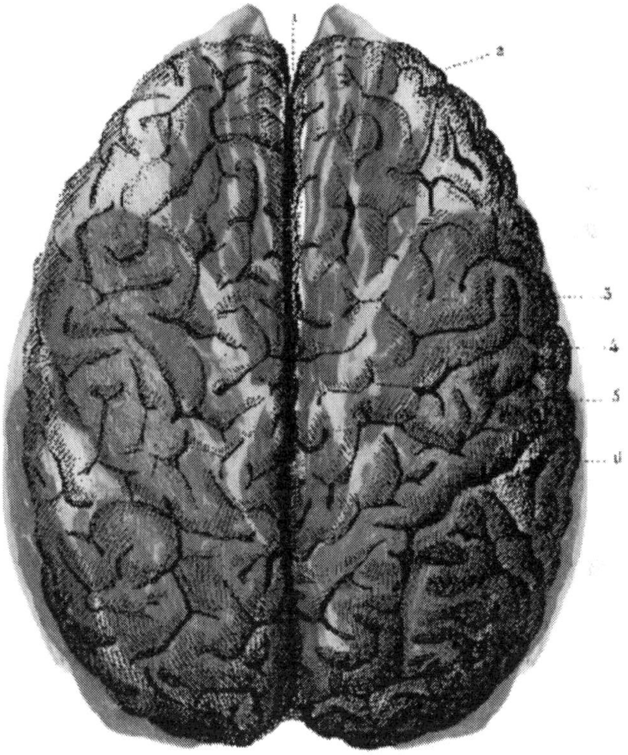
2
3
4
5

72. Another Bullet in the Echo Chamber

9.5.24

There's a popular theory that we are living in a civilized society. I think there are a lot of holes in that theory. They're bullet holes. Humanity is a staggering and tragically sad disappointment. The news is another knot in the throat of anyone with any compassion.

There's nothing civil about our civilization.

73. This Mindset Will Self-Destruct in…

9.10.24

Beautifully rare are individuals who endure adversity, oppression, and misfortune beyond most of our imaginations and yet are somehow still able to express remorse for the struggles of others. However, there is no greater or more misplaced arrogance than that of a person who believes their suffering is more valid than everyone else's. This is the suck of self-absorption. This is the thinking of a person destined to drown in self-pity. This, above all else, is the mindset that needs to be altered before one can even attempt to seek a glimpse of hope. The sneaking idea that no one can understand what you've been through is not only incorrect, it is the offense by which a self-fulfilling prophecy of emptiness and loneliness is propagated. It is the map by which to find the imaginary isolation one creates for oneself in one's own mind. Tell people they couldn't possibly understand or empathize enough, and you will become the reason they choose not to show you how wrong you are. Perhaps there is an untainted soul among us who has lived a life so enchanted that they may not be able to relate, but trust that they are very few if they exist at all. By allowing yourself to believe they are everywhere—everyone, you will only ostracize yourself from those who might offer you true understanding and compassion.

THIS MESSAGE WILL SELF-DESTRUCT IN...

74. Stoop-idity

9.17.24

"If I have to listen to one more adult say, 'But they did it first,' about anything, my brain is going to implode and drain out of my nose. Aside from being wildly obnoxious, it's way too motivated. You don't have to do things because other people do things. In fact, you don't have to do a lot of things. Stop doing things, people!"

-Joseph D. Newcomer – The Unmotivational Life Coach

If you're basing the amount of integrity you're willing to have on how much integrity you think others have, you didn't have any to begin with.

Whataboutisms and but-they-did-it-firsts and the-end-justifies-the-means-es are all useless deflections proving only that in the face of scrutiny, you will easily succumb to the lowest level of others—stooping to their stupidity.

75. The Regrettably Unlived Moments at the End of Time

10.1.24

I have an overwhelming suspicion that at the end of our lives—at the end of existence as a whole, above all the mortal pursuits on which we so desperately and painstakingly focused, we will wish we'd focused, instead, on fucking off and fucking around. When I truly take the time to consider everything, I can't think of anything more important or enjoyable than taking my kid to the movies or an amusement park and laughing.

76. Should've Eaten My Vegetables

11.6.24

I think one of the biggest issues we face is the fact that we're constantly comparing ourselves to people who can afford to pay other people to handle all the stressful bullshit life throws at us. It's pretty obvious that not having to do dishes or pay bills or go grocery shopping would make you feel and look a hell of a lot younger. I mean, when do you think the last time Jennifer Aniston had to call customer service was? I haven't seen any studies on this, but I'm pretty sure that one phone call to customer service ages you at least three years. We should be comparing ourselves to something that sets a more attainable standard. Like maybe the produce we bought last weekend. The vegetables that are now a brown, drippy, wilted mess in the bottom drawer of the fridge, where they sat untouched since we bought them, because ordering a pizza was way easier than having to take shit out, prepare it, and cook after a long day of the life being sucked out of you by everything.

Maybe I'm looking a little rough these days, but I probably don't look as bad as limp, moldy celery.

CENSORED

77. Man-ipulation by Athazagoraphobia

11.19.24

Our biggest issues are zealotry and extremism based on our highly manipulable fear of losing even the most insignificant and illusory amount of power we believe ourselves to have. It's used to pull us to the edges on both sides of every issue, and, en masse, we allow it to. To secure our loyalty, our worst fears are exploited. Radicalization is the side effect, and we are happily running toward the fringes.

On a more positive note, we've achieved a seemingly impossible feat of contortion and managed to stick our heads squarely up our own asses.

78. CON-Fidence

12.3.24

If you find yourself exhausted from having to constantly defend someone or something, it may be time to start questioning whether or not you should be.

That's way too much work, especially if you're just wrong.

Also, it's okay to be wrong, but the longer you are and the more fiercely you defend it makes it all that much more difficult to be forgiven for it.

Be as open to understanding things you'd rather not believe as you are drawn to those you wish were true. Reserve the greatest amount of your suspicion for those who regale you with confirmation and validation that you are right about everything you believe-everything you suspect. While it's a distinctly easy thing to delight in, you're not right about everything, and anyone telling you otherwise stands to gain something from lying to you about it.

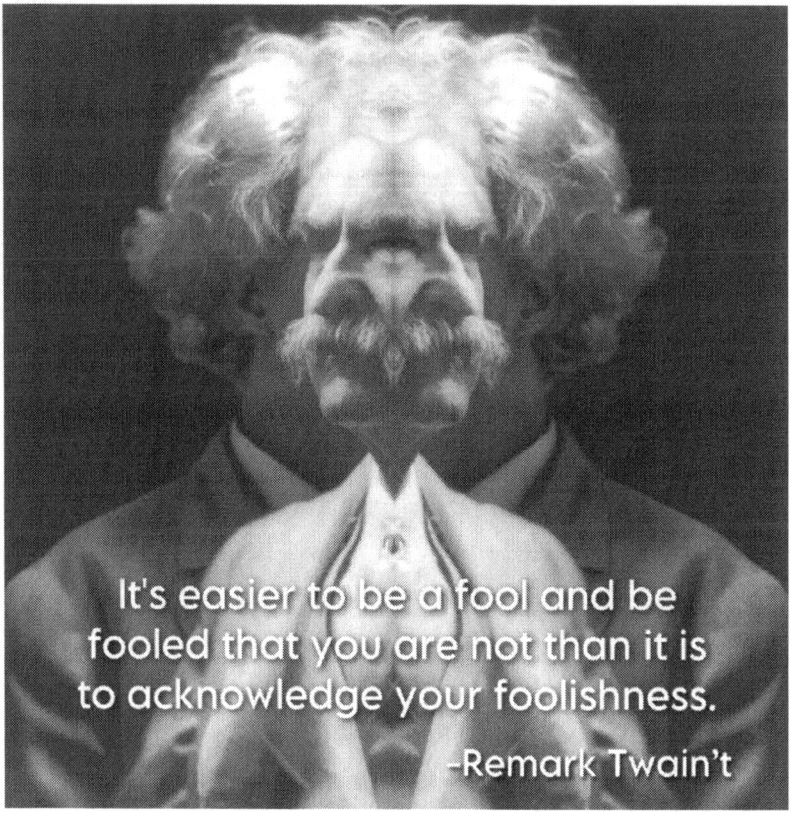
It's easier to be a fool and be
fooled that you are not than it is
to acknowledge your foolishness.
-Remark Twain't

79. The Mandela Deflect

12.10.24

Modern thought would have us label Nelson Mandela a virtue-signaling narcissist. Do you remember when virtue-signaling was just called kindness and standing up for people? Now we tell each other to stop being offended for other people. Really? Jeez, I bet there are a lot of bullied, abused, and dead people throughout history who wish(ed) people were more offended for them sooner. I would imagine the people in the concentration and internment camps would've hoped more people were offended for them a hell of a lot sooner. It would probably be pretty helpful now if more people were virtue-signaling to stop school shootings.

You can drown in a mere teaspoon of water, but I don't think any of us are in any danger of drowning in the depths of humanity's character. It's hardly enough to call it a drop.

"Kill them with kindness" is now "kill those with kindness."

80. Manifest Extremity

12.17.24

We believe things into being—into existence—into reality. Not that they're any more real than they ever were but for only in the popular opinion. It's as close as we come to actual manifestation, but it is close enough to allow those clutching their crystals, their rosaries, and/or their pearls to dictate the standards of our society. If enough people believe in something hard enough for long enough, the rest of us will be forced to endure the absurdity of whatever malformed concept the masses decide is the truth.

The blurred vision on the horizon has come into focus—its clarity unburdened by the fact that it is merely a mirage.

81. Contradiction Bias

2025 Previously Unpublished

Confirmation Bias can be strong, but it doesn't match the absolutely cementing validation of Contradiction Bias. When someone vehemently and insultingly disagrees with something totally reasonable that I've said on social media, I sometimes investigate their profiles to figure out who I'm dealing with. I almost always find that they've alienated everyone in their lives and are frequent sharers of ignorant, misinformed drivel, and I feel a whole lot more satisfied with the conclusions I've drawn than when someone or something simply agrees with me.

Sometimes, finding someone who disagrees with you is more validating than finding someone who agrees.

82. Avarice Found

2025 Previously Unpublished

No one has any integrity, so why should I?

This is the nonsensical slogan of the modern age. It's always been part of the collective consciousness, but never has it been so prevalent in all aspects of society. It's hypocrisy gone stupid—not for the sake of irony or satire, but just for lack of understanding—ignorance. Every day, it becomes less of an excuse and more of a "reason"—its validity strengthening in our misguided opinions while its merit is truly no greater than it ever was. We no longer see the shame in its flawed logic—the true definition of the word lost forever. Though we feel a great sense of tragedy in the loss of what it once was, for our stupidity and ignorance, we are unable to connect the subconscious reason to the mutual sense of loss.

83. Bad Actors in Good Faith

2025 Previously Unpublished

Look, you don't need to be smart, and honestly, for most of us, that's not really even an option. You just need to be smart enough to know that there are things you aren't smart enough to know and that there are other people who are smart enough to know them.

Specialization has been, and remains, one of the driving forces behind the evolution of our society. If we don't trust and/or are unable to trust people who are experts in their specialized fields of study (who, mind you, are not always right but are more often so than someone with no expertise, give or take a few bad actors), as a civilization, we devolve.

84. The Hier-Archaic and the Needy

2025 Previously Unpublished

Most of us have heard about or seen Maslow's Hierarchy of Needs. If you haven't, the basic idea is that the human experience relies on specific building blocks to achieve a meaningful, self-actualized existence.

The first level is having our basic needs met—food, shelter, water, etc. Next, we need safety and security—job, health, family, social ability, etc. Then, we need to have a sense of love and belonging. Self-esteem is the final stage before reaching the pinnacle of existence- self-actualization—morality, creativity, purpose, and so on.

When we're taught this, it's generally used as a motivational roadmap to success, despite its obvious and overlooked flaws, and to some degree, it makes some sense. It makes more sense if you understand where it came from.

You see, later in life, our friend Maslow was a bit more vocal about his thoughts on society and politics. He began voicing his belief that we should operate under two forms of government simultaneously. One form of government would resemble our current system, serving to police the general population. The second form of government would be self-governance, which would apply exclusively to "Elites." People of high standing, stature in society, and wealth wouldn't be beholden to the laws the rest of us need to follow for our own good, as they obviously know better than we or the government about what needs to be accomplished. Any limitations on them would be detrimental to the greater good. It wasn't a particularly favored concept.

Knowing how he actually felt changes how we should interpret his Hierarchy of Needs. Turns out, he was really just trying to tell everyone that if you're poor and you weren't brought up in an affluent environment, you really cannot experience self-actualization—that you are generally lesser than and in need of external governance. Obviously, this is a horrible and absurd way to view the human experience, but if you stop and think about it, no matter how disgusting it is, this is how our society operates. We see the evidence of "Elites" operating nearly completely guardrail-less with no discernible set of ethics or moral code. The laws that apply to you and me are overlooked for those who Maslow would consider "Elites."

It seems as though, while people in positions of power panned his idea, secretly, they embraced it. And now, this is where we are and have been for quite some time. I think the current state of affairs is just the next step in a series of slips down the slope to Maslow's "Elites" being brazenly transparent about their already evident ability to ignore all the rules of society by which the rest of us need abide or be punished.

85. AntiSocial MEdia

2025 Previously Unpublished

Social media didn't make people worse. It just allows them to assume their true identities because they don't feel there will be any repercussions for their actions when they're online. This is just who they've always been. We should probably actually thank social media for showing us who people truly are. The person who said that terrible thing online is the person who's been thinking it all along.

86. Immoral Majority

2025 Previously Unpublished

If you've ever needed the government or laws or religion to help you to be a moral and decent human or to control your impulses to deviate from simple human kindness, you probably weren't a decent human being to begin with and are most likely doing a poor job of adhering to chosen codes of conduct anyway.

At this point, what's been made socially acceptable—what's been championed by the self-appointed "moral majority" is no more refined than absolute savagery. There isn't a species of wild animal with less civility than those who feign to have a stronghold on the moral high ground. Anarchy promotes more responsibility than these principles that have been so perverted they've lost all of the very little meaning they ever had.

We are all now only destined to reap the ironies of hypocrisy.

87. In Validation

2025 Previously Unpublished

People are so concerned about everyone getting desensitized to things. For the most part, I think it's a little over-exaggerated, but there is one thing people are becoming desensitized to, and I think we should be a lot more concerned about it.

Stupidity... It's unavoidable.

We see it everywhere we look and so consistently that we've all but given up pointing it out. Now, when someone says the most dangerously stupid shit, everyone goes, "Well, everyone is entitled to their opinion." And some of this ridiculous crap is coming from people who make important decisions that affect millions of people. But by all means, let's keep validating their absolute ignorance and stupidity while these idiots design atrocities so detrimentally dumb and on such a grand scale that they can't be fixed, and honestly, we, as a society, are most likely already well beyond that point.

88. Minding the Hive

2025 Previously Unpublished

America has a beehive hanging from its neck. Everyone wants to be rid of it, but a lot of people on both sides are hitting it with sticks, ignorantly believing this will somehow fix things, or perhaps simply for the satisfaction of creating action over stagnation. But you can't fix chaos with more chaos, and we can no longer ignore the swarming entropy.

89. Panderer-in-Chief

2025 Previously Unpublished

On a long enough timeline, it's impossible to please both the fans and the sponsors. Making decisions solely based on one or the other isn't any better. Deciding not to pander to one or the other or futilely attempting to play both sides will get you nowhere, regardless of how right or important it is to do so.

All of this is why integrity is all but obsolete and rarely, if ever, wins out. When you pledge your allegiance to a school of thought and agree to agree to all of its tenets, regardless of their merit, you espouse this reality for better or worse—unconditionally, and unconditional support of anything divorces us from the reason and accountability needed to make good choices.

Even when you support something on a grand scale, you should still debate the minutiae when any part of it flies in the face of what you hold to be true. This is the difficulty of populist politics. The most popular option is rarely the best option, and many times, it's much closer to the worst.

In a reasonably equally divided nation, by choosing a champion through populism, what we've truly and proactively selected is the person who is more willing to forgo their personal beliefs and integrity to amass a majority of our support. The design demands the office be filled by the unscrupulous, leaving many of us to wonder how we've ended up here, thoroughly disappointed not only for opposite reasons, but also for the same offense that those we chose aren't doing what they said they would. For worse or for worst, these are the empty promises made in the pursuit of garnering popularity.

90. Somewhere Over the Distorted Illusion

2025 Previously Unpublished

I just read a quote that said, "You have to look through the rain to see the rainbow." I assume they meant to try to see beyond your problems and find a way to appreciate life. But when you see a rainbow, you're looking at the rain, not through it. If you looked through it, you would just see a distorted, illusory version of what was on the other side.

Maybe a more accurate statement, such as "You have to look at the rain to see a rainbow," would make more sense. I suppose acknowledging your problems instead of pretending they aren't there would probably make life a little better. Still, the even bigger issue is that rainbows are just optical illusions anyway. So, what you're really saying is happiness is an illusion, which makes a ton of sense, but I doubt that's what anyone who would say this type of thing intends.

Maybe I'm overthinking it, but also maybe they're underthinking it.

91. The Incapable Ableist

2025 Previously Unpublished

There are a million sayings about excuses being unacceptable, but most of the people who say them fail to recognize that a legitimate excuse is actually called a reason. For those individuals, I would like to share that there's also a word for failing to recognize reason, and that word is unreasonable. You may want to consider that maybe people aren't making excuses—maybe you and your dumb sayings are just unreasonable.

92. The Socio Path to Empathy

2025 Previously Unpublished

Intelligence is empathy and nothing more. Though you may not support, though you may even adamantly disagree, the ability to comprehend another person's reasoning is the only thing that creates a civilized society. Without it, we all end up a disjointed smattering of narcissists and sociopaths who all need to be cared for by someone empathetic enough to do so, but without anyone left who is able to.

93. Blatant Latency

2025 Previously Unpublished

Some days, I just wish I had something to say that was a little more esoteric and nuanced about the direction in which society is going, but it's all just blatant and apparent and obvious. There's nothing so difficult to understand or delicate about it that it would require any amount of diplomatic eloquence. The fact of the matter is quite simple—shit's just getting really fucking stupid, and there's really not a better or more accurate way to say it. Yet, some people continue to pretend not to understand.

I guess the thing I wish I could impress upon those people the most is that if you are being willfully ignorant about what's been happening—if you're pretending not to understand or believe the reality of what's clearly happening, you're no longer pretending to be stupid. You just are.

94. See You at the Bottom

2025 Previously Unpublished

It's hard to watch people believe one thing could be the solution to all of our problems when, throughout history, anytime anyone believed that to be the case, it ended in absolute tragedy. Between optimism and total disregard for our past missteps, there's a line, and it appears to be fine from a certain illusory perspective. It's not a fine line, though. It's a canyon carved by centuries of pain, loss, and woe, and we are stumbling off its cliffs.

95. The Paradigm Shift of the Surreal

2025 Previously Unpublished

I keep having these dreams that are so simplistic and ordinary that they hardly resemble the dreams I'm accustomed to having. I had a dream about being really upset because my brand-new shower curtain ripped. I think reality's become so twisted that my brain is attempting to satiate its need for boring, mundane normalcy in my dreams. My brain is compensating for the need to see things that are not entirely surreal. It's as if we are living in a reality created entirely of a crude and disturbing version of Salvador Dali art, and my mind is painting abstracts from the perspective of that reality, so the paintings are just realistic landscapes and bowls of fruit, and I wonder if others are having similar subconscious lives.

96. The Hot Seat

2025 Previously Unpublished

Life is like a warm seat in a public restroom. Some of us are hovering because we don't even want to think about it. Some of us sit and obliviously enjoy the warmth. Some of us sit because we're old, tired, and have no other choice, and we find the heat nauseating because we know how it got to this point. Some of us won't even go into the restroom because we're aware of the horrors that await, and we end up ruining some underwear trying to get home to the sanctity of our own bathrooms. The rest of us don't notice because we're busy wiping poo on the walls.

Also by Joseph D. Newcomer

El Camino Blue

Diminishing Return

Thought & Other Absurdities

Darkest Day

Fucking Relax: A Journal for Mental Well-Being

Children's Books

Let's Make S'mores

Ari and The Armpit Mouse

Find his titles at deadstarpress.com, amazon.com, and many other places the Internet takes you.

ABOUT THE AUTHOR

Joseph D. Newcomer is a writer of literary, speculative fiction, and social commentary and the founder & owner of Dead Star Press.

His writing can be found at deadstarpress.com, in the Thought & Other Absurdities blog at josephdnewcomer.com, and on social media as the Unmotivational Life Coach.

He can be found buying comic books and watching sci-fi films and shows with the greatest loves of his life, his daughter, Ariella Nova Newcomer, and his incredibly more significant other, Andrea Greenwald.

Someday, he hopes to be sucked into The Twilight Zone, though he suspects we already were.

Made in the USA
Coppell, TX
05 April 2026

74818396R00111